My dear Rose,

Here I am with Fox, traveling through the stars on the trail of the Snake. We just left Zephyr and Foehn on the planet of the Eolians. Thanks to them, I've learned that we must always encourage the ones we love to follow not our dreams but their own.

I'm sorry, but I'll have to leave you now. Another star system is on the point of being destroyed. The Snake has wasted no time! Now it seems he's on the planet of the Firebird… Fox is going to like that!

This journey is long, and we're so far away from you… I think about you every day when I watch the sunset. And you, my Rose, what are you dreaming of?

The Little Prince

First American edition published in 2012 by Graphic Universe™.

Le Petit Prince ™

based on the masterpiece by Antoine de Saint-Exupéry

© 2012 LPPM
An animated series based on the novel *Le Petit Prince* by Antoine de Saint-Exupéry
Developed for television by Matthieu Delaporte, Alexandre de la Patellière, and Bertrand Gatignol
Directed by Pierre-Alain Chartier

© 2012 ÉDITIONS GLÉNAT
Copyright © 2012 by Lerner Publishing Group, Inc., for the current edition

Graphic Universe™
A division of Lerner Publishing Group, Inc.
241 First Avenue North
Minneapolis, MN 55401 U.S.A.

Website address: www.lernerbooks.com

Library of Congress Cataloging-in-Publication Data

Dorison, Guillaume.
　　[Planète de L'Oiseau de Feu. English]
　　The planet of the Firebird / by Julien Magnat ; adapted by Guillaume Dorison ; based on the masterpiece by Antoine de Saint-Exupéry ; illustrated by Élyum Studio, Diane Fayolle, and Jérôme Benoit ; translation, Carol Klio Burrell. — 1st American ed.
　　　p.　cm. — (The little prince ; #02)
　　ISBN: 978—0—7613—8752—7 (lib. bdg. : alk. paper)
　　1. Graphic novels. I. Fayolle, Diane. II. Benoit, Jérôme. III. Saint-Exupéry, Antoine de, 1900—1944. Petit Prince. IV. Élyum Studio. V. Petit Prince (Television program) VI. Title.
PZ7.7.D67Pk 2012
741.5'944—dc23   2011047659

Manufactured in the United States of America
1 — DP — 7/15/12

THE NEW ADVENTURES
BASED ON THE MASTERPIECE BY ANTOINE DE SAINT-EXUPÉRY

The Little Prince

THE PLANET OF THE FIREBIRD

Based on the animated series and an original story by Julien Magnat

Design: Élyum Studio
Adaptation: Guillaume Dorison
Artistic Direction: Didier Poli
Art: Diane Fayolle
Backgrounds: Jérôme Benoit
Coloring: Digikore
Editing: Didier Poli
Editorial Consultant: Didier Convard

Translation: Carol Burrell

Graphic Universe™ · Minneapolis · New York

⭐ THE LITTLE PRINCE

The Little Prince has extraordinary gifts. His sense of wonder allows him to discover what no one else can see. The Little Prince can communicate with all the beings in the universe, even the animals and plants. His powers grow over the course of his adventures.

The Prince's uniform:
When he wears the uniform of a prince, he is more agile and quick. When faced with difficult situations, the Little Prince also carries a sword that lets him sketch and bring to life anything from his imagination.

His sketchbook:
When he is not in his Prince's clothing, the Little Prince carries a sketchbook. When he blows on the pages, they take wing and form objects that he'll find very useful.

⭐ FOX

A grouch, a trickster, and, so he says, interested only in his next meal, Fox is in reality the Little Prince's best friend. As such, he is always there to give him help, but also just as much to help him to grow and to learn about the world.

⭐ THE SNAKE

Even though the Little Prince still does not know exactly why, there can be no doubt that the Snake has set his mind to plunging the entire universe into darkness! And to accomplish his goal, this malicious being is ready to use any form of deception. However, the Snake never takes action himself. He prefers to bring out the wickedness in those beings he has chosen to bite, tempting them to put their own worlds in danger.

⭐ THE GLOOMIES

When people who have been "bitten" by the Snake have completely destroyed their own planets, they become Gloomies, slaves to their Snake master. The Gloomies act as a group and carry out the Serpent's most vile orders so as to get the better of the Little Prince!

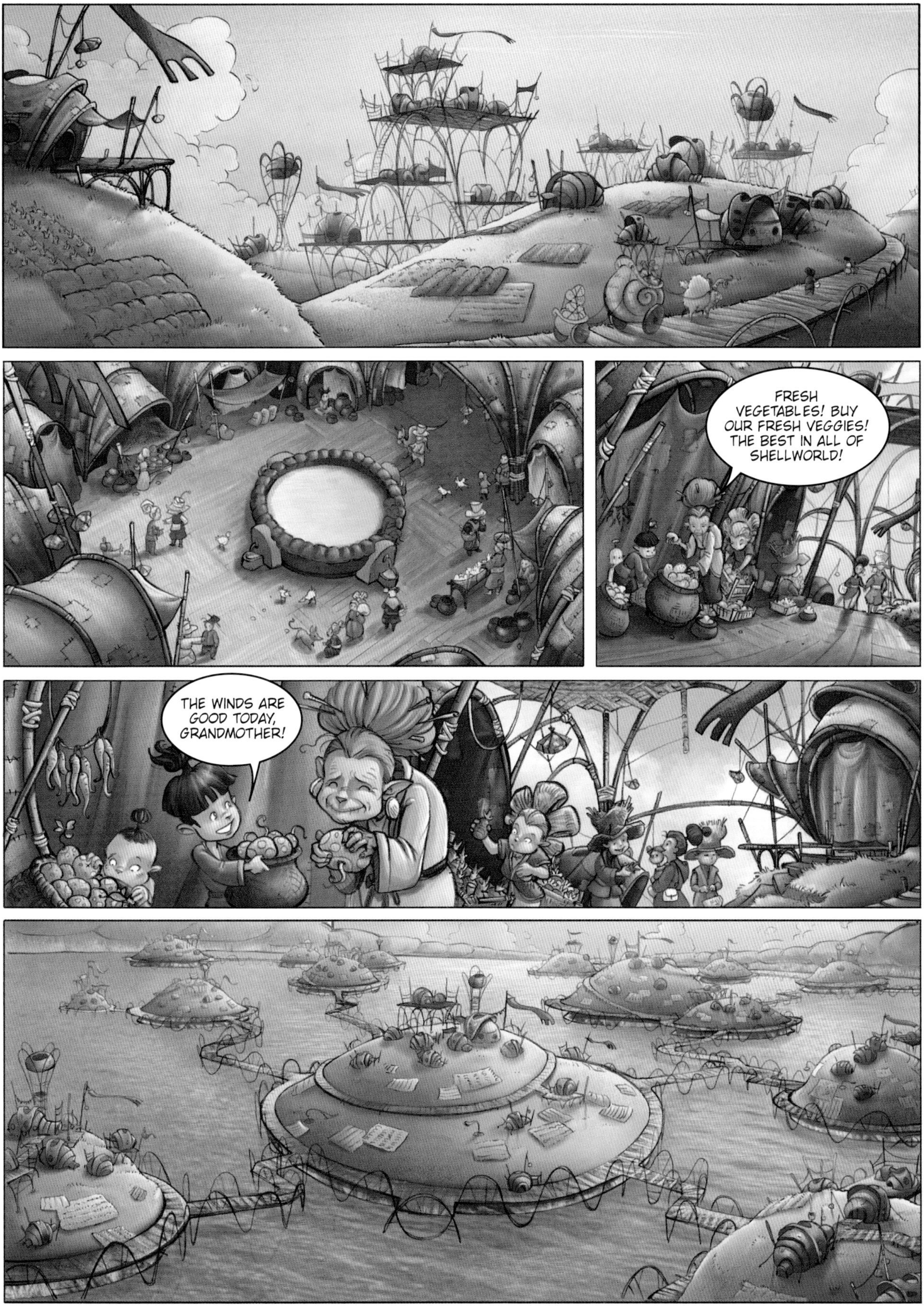
FRESH VEGETABLES! BUY OUR FRESH VEGGIES! THE BEST IN ALL OF SHELLWORLD!
THE WINDS ARE GOOD TODAY, GRANDMOTHER!

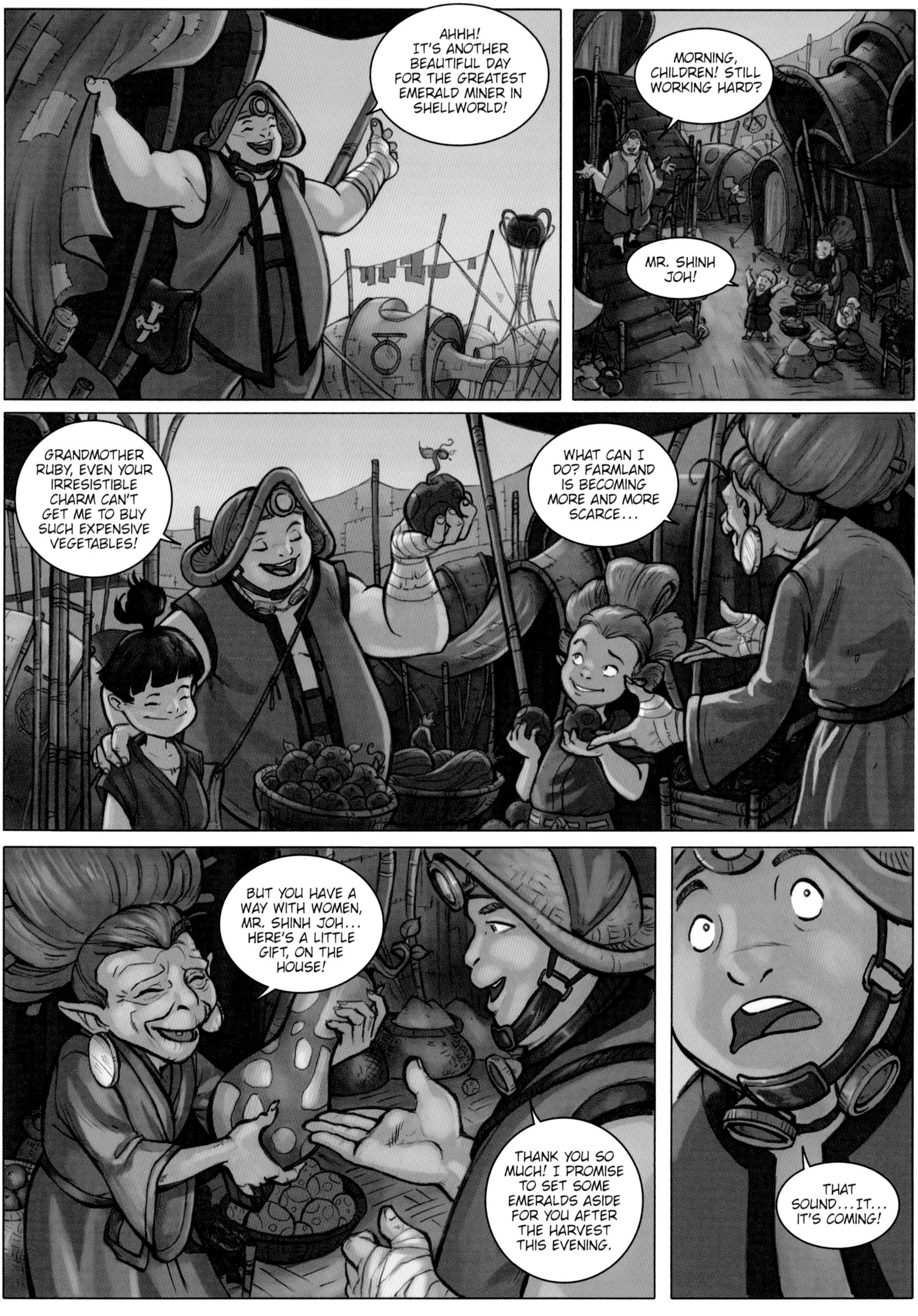
AHHH! IT'S ANOTHER BEAUTIFUL DAY FOR THE GREATEST EMERALD MINER IN SHELLWORLD!
MORNING, CHILDREN! STILL WORKING HARD?
MR. SHINH JOH!
GRANDMOTHER RUBY, EVEN YOUR IRRESISTIBLE CHARM CAN'T GET ME TO BUY SUCH EXPENSIVE VEGETABLES!
WHAT CAN I DO? FARMLAND IS BECOMING MORE AND MORE SCARCE...
BUT YOU HAVE A WAY WITH WOMEN, MR. SHINH JOH... HERE'S A LITTLE GIFT, ON THE HOUSE!
THANK YOU SO MUCH! I PROMISE TO SET SOME EMERALDS ASIDE FOR YOU AFTER THE HARVEST THIS EVENING.
THAT SOUND...IT... IT'S COMING!

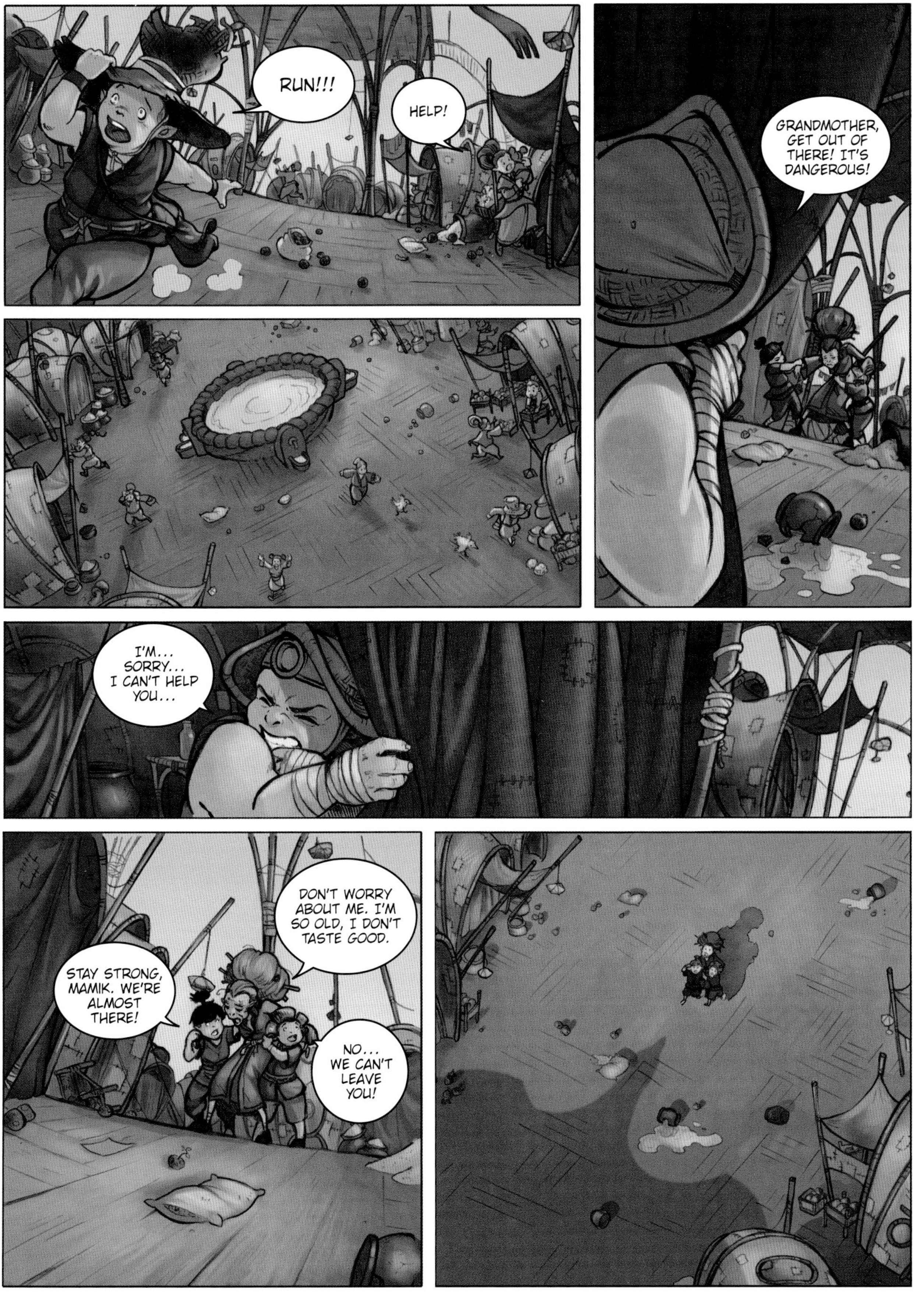
RUN!!!
HELP!
GRANDMOTHER, GET OUT OF THERE! IT'S DANGEROUS!
I'M... SORRY... I CAN'T HELP YOU...
STAY STRONG, MAMIK. WE'RE ALMOST THERE!
DON'T WORRY ABOUT ME. I'M SO OLD, I DON'T TASTE GOOD.
NO... WE CAN'T LEAVE YOU!

GOOD, NO SNAKE HERE AND NOTHING TO EAT. CAN WE GO NOW?

IF ONLY YOU DIDN'T HAVE THIS BAD HABIT OF WANTING TO SAVE THE UNIVERSE...BUT WHAT'S THAT?

THERE ARE NO SIGNS OF LIFE, FOX. MAYBE WE'RE ALREADY TOO LATE!

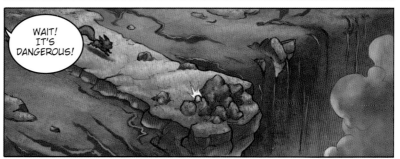

WAIT! IT'S DANGEROUS!

WATCH OUT, FOX!

UMMMPHHH... WITH THIS, I'LL BE ABLE TO BUY MYSELF A WHOLE CHICKEN!

6

BLAH BLAH BLAH. WE ALWAYS HAVE TO DO WHAT HIS HIGHNESS THE LITTLE PRINCE WANTS! HELP THIS PLANET, THAT STRANGER, HIS ROSE, ETC. AND WHAT ABOUT **ME?**

I'LL FINALLY BE PAID BACK FOR ALL MY EFFORTS AND...

WHOOOAAA!

THE PORTAL IS OUT OF REACH. WE'RE TRAPPED BY THE LAVA!

UH...YOU KNOW YOU'RE MY HERO, RIGHT? AND...COULD YOU TAKE OUT YOUR MAGIC NOTEBOOK?

LOOK UP THERE! I HAVE A BETTER IDEA.

WE'RE SAVED!

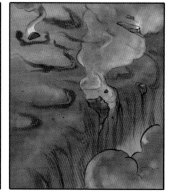

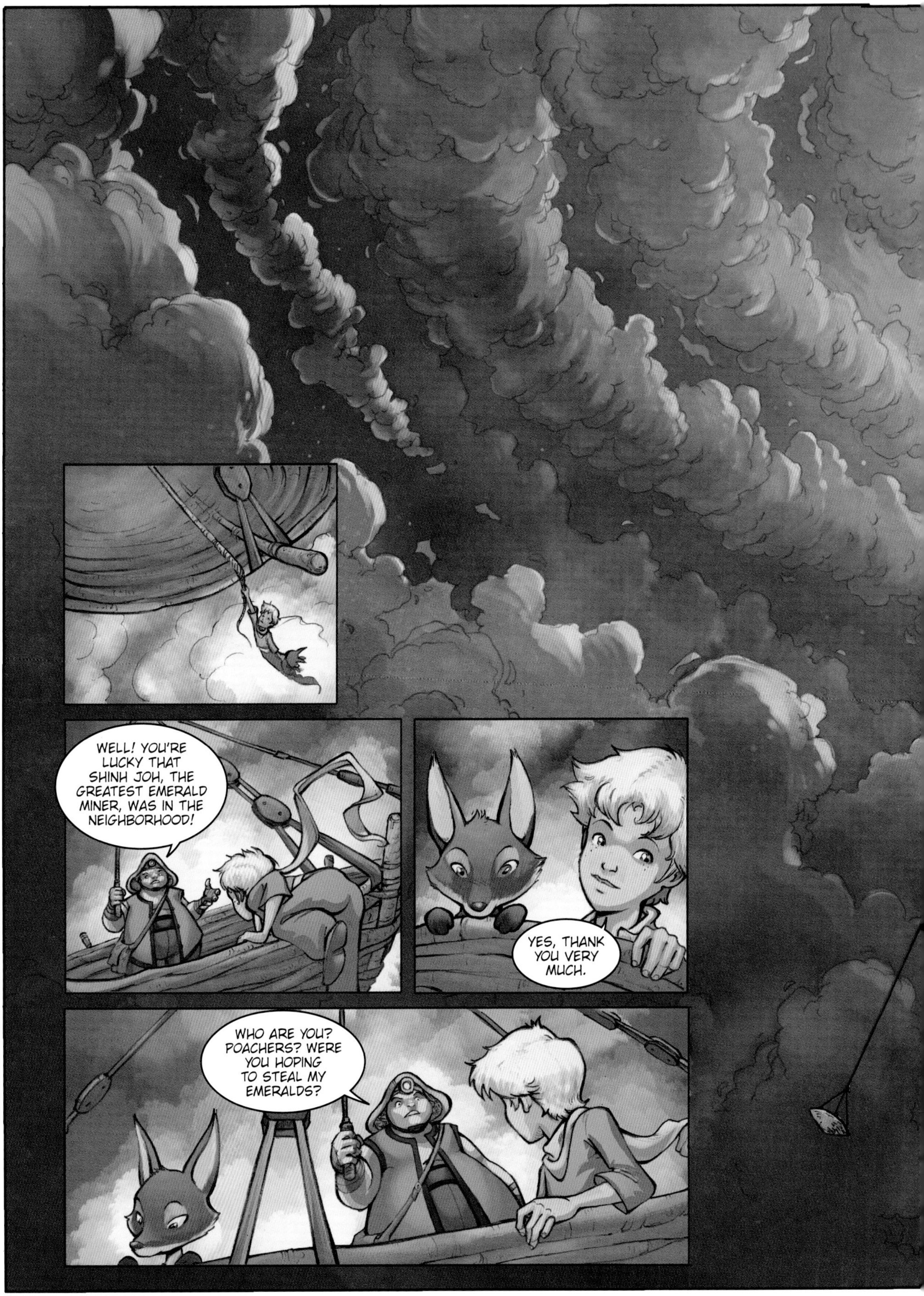
WELL! YOU'RE LUCKY THAT SHINH JOH, THE GREATEST EMERALD MINER, WAS IN THE NEIGHBORHOOD!
YES, THANK YOU VERY MUCH.
WHO ARE YOU? POACHERS? WERE YOU HOPING TO STEAL MY EMERALDS?

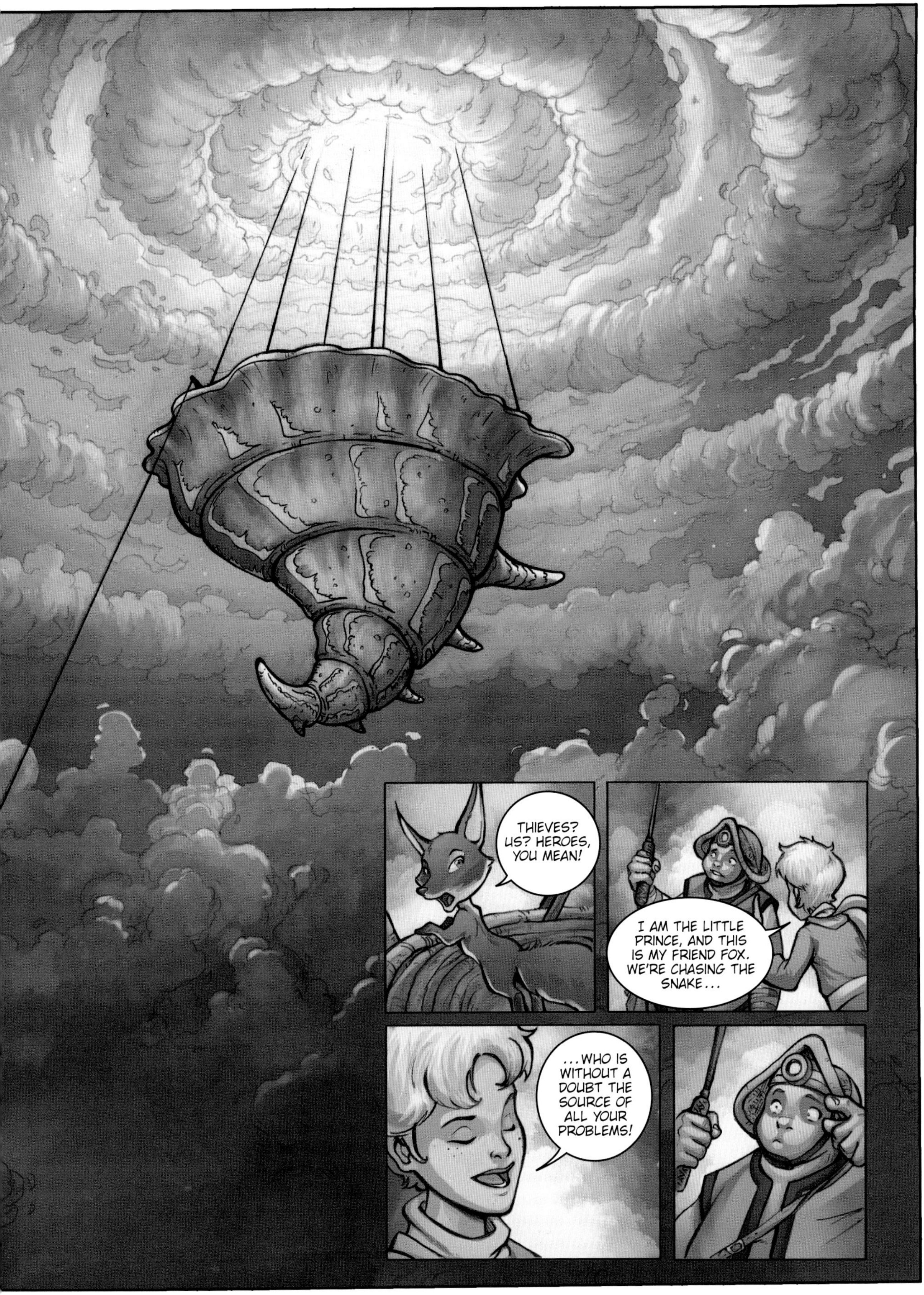
THIEVES? US? HEROES, YOU MEAN!
I AM THE LITTLE PRINCE, AND THIS IS MY FRIEND FOX. WE'RE CHASING THE SNAKE...
...WHO IS WITHOUT A DOUBT THE SOURCE OF ALL YOUR PROBLEMS!

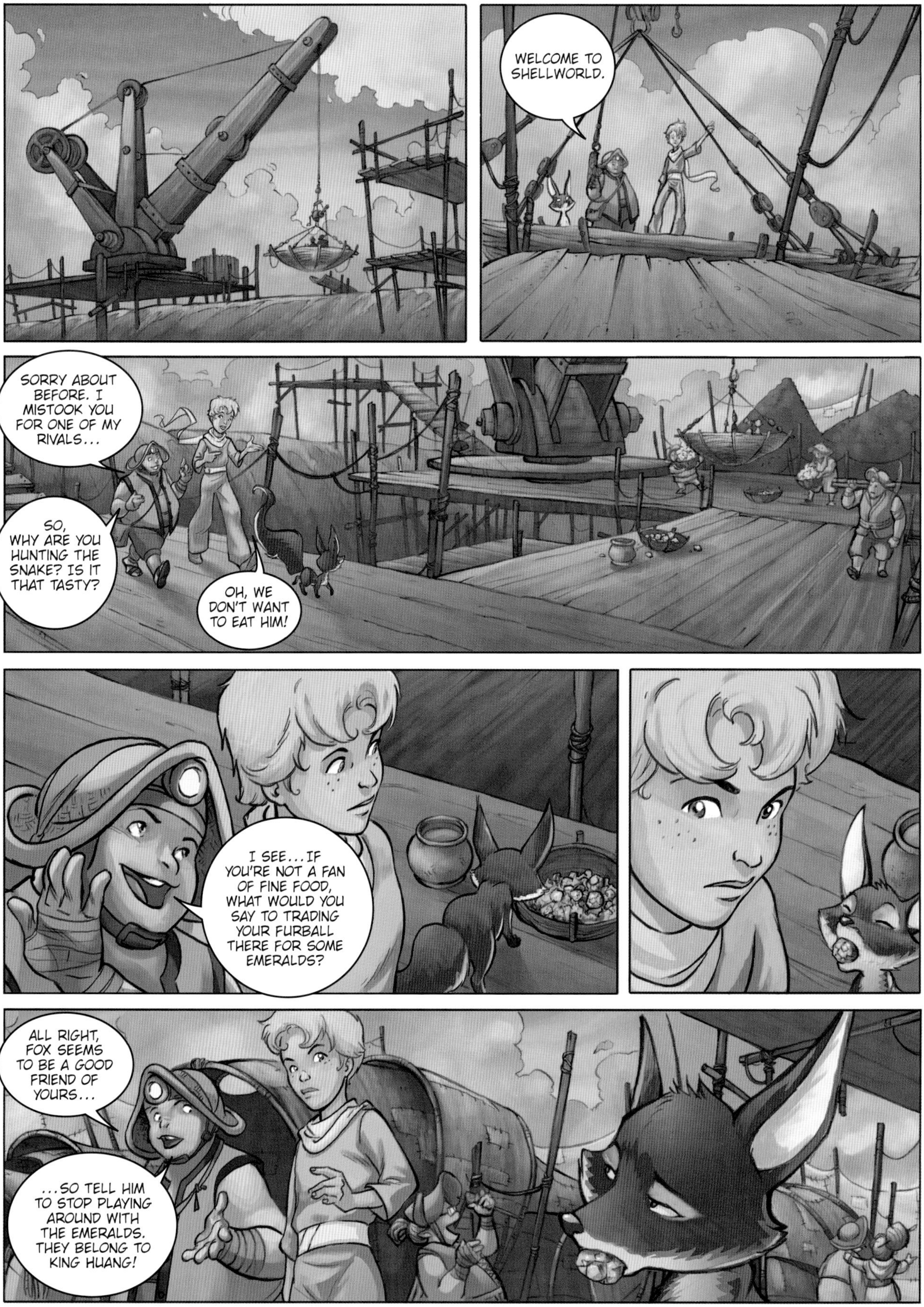
WELCOME TO SHELLWORLD.
SORRY ABOUT BEFORE. I MISTOOK YOU FOR ONE OF MY RIVALS...
SO, WHY ARE YOU HUNTING THE SNAKE? IS IT THAT TASTY?
OH, WE DON'T WANT TO EAT HIM!
I SEE... IF YOU'RE NOT A FAN OF FINE FOOD, WHAT WOULD YOU SAY TO TRADING YOUR FURBALL THERE FOR SOME EMERALDS?
ALL RIGHT, FOX SEEMS TO BE A GOOD FRIEND OF YOURS...
...SO TELL HIM TO STOP PLAYING AROUND WITH THE EMERALDS. THEY BELONG TO KING HUANG!

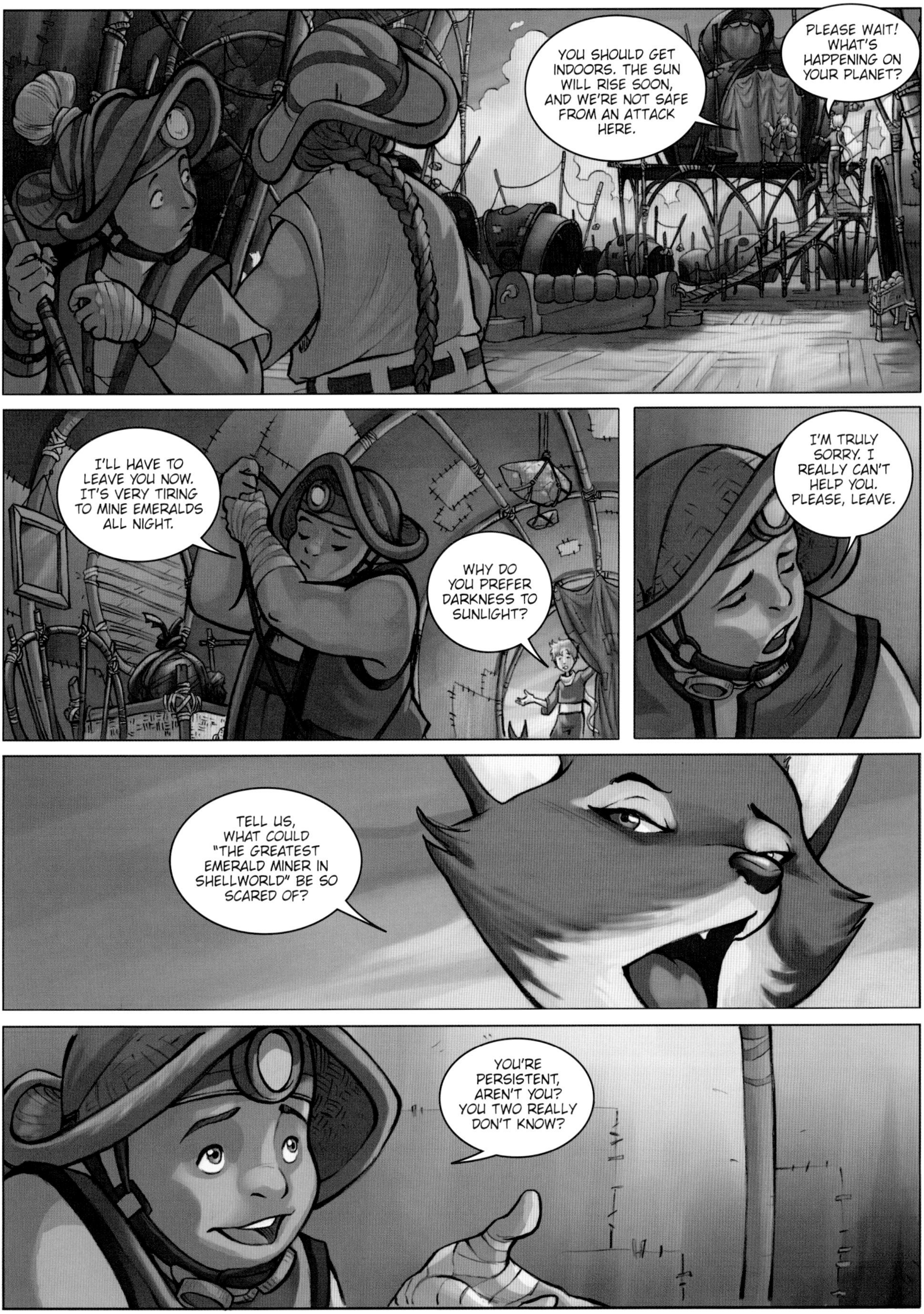
YOU SHOULD GET INDOORS. THE SUN WILL RISE SOON, AND WE'RE NOT SAFE FROM AN ATTACK HERE.
PLEASE WAIT! WHAT'S HAPPENING ON YOUR PLANET?
I'LL HAVE TO LEAVE YOU NOW. IT'S VERY TIRING TO MINE EMERALDS ALL NIGHT.
WHY DO YOU PREFER DARKNESS TO SUNLIGHT?
I'M TRULY SORRY. I REALLY CAN'T HELP YOU. PLEASE, LEAVE.
TELL US, WHAT COULD "THE GREATEST EMERALD MINER IN SHELLWORLD" BE SO SCARED OF?
YOU'RE PERSISTENT, AREN'T YOU? YOU TWO REALLY DON'T KNOW?

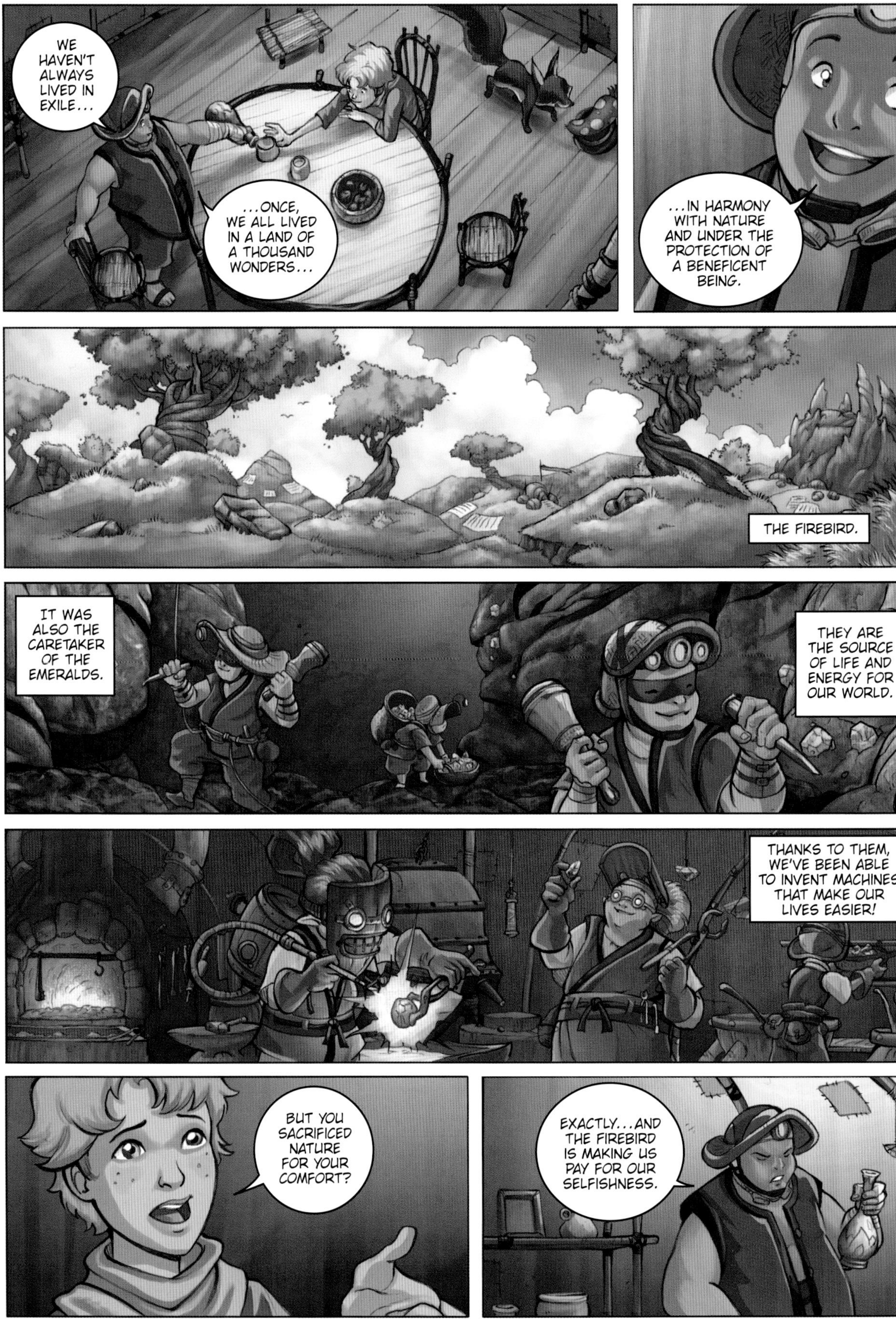
WE HAVEN'T ALWAYS LIVED IN EXILE...
...ONCE, WE ALL LIVED IN A LAND OF A THOUSAND WONDERS...
...IN HARMONY WITH NATURE AND UNDER THE PROTECTION OF A BENEFICENT BEING.
THE FIREBIRD.
IT WAS ALSO THE CARETAKER OF THE EMERALDS.
THEY ARE THE SOURCE OF LIFE AND ENERGY FOR OUR WORLD.
THANKS TO THEM, WE'VE BEEN ABLE TO INVENT MACHINES THAT MAKE OUR LIVES EASIER!
BUT YOU SACRIFICED NATURE FOR YOUR COMFORT?
EXACTLY...AND THE FIREBIRD IS MAKING US PAY FOR OUR SELFISHNESS.

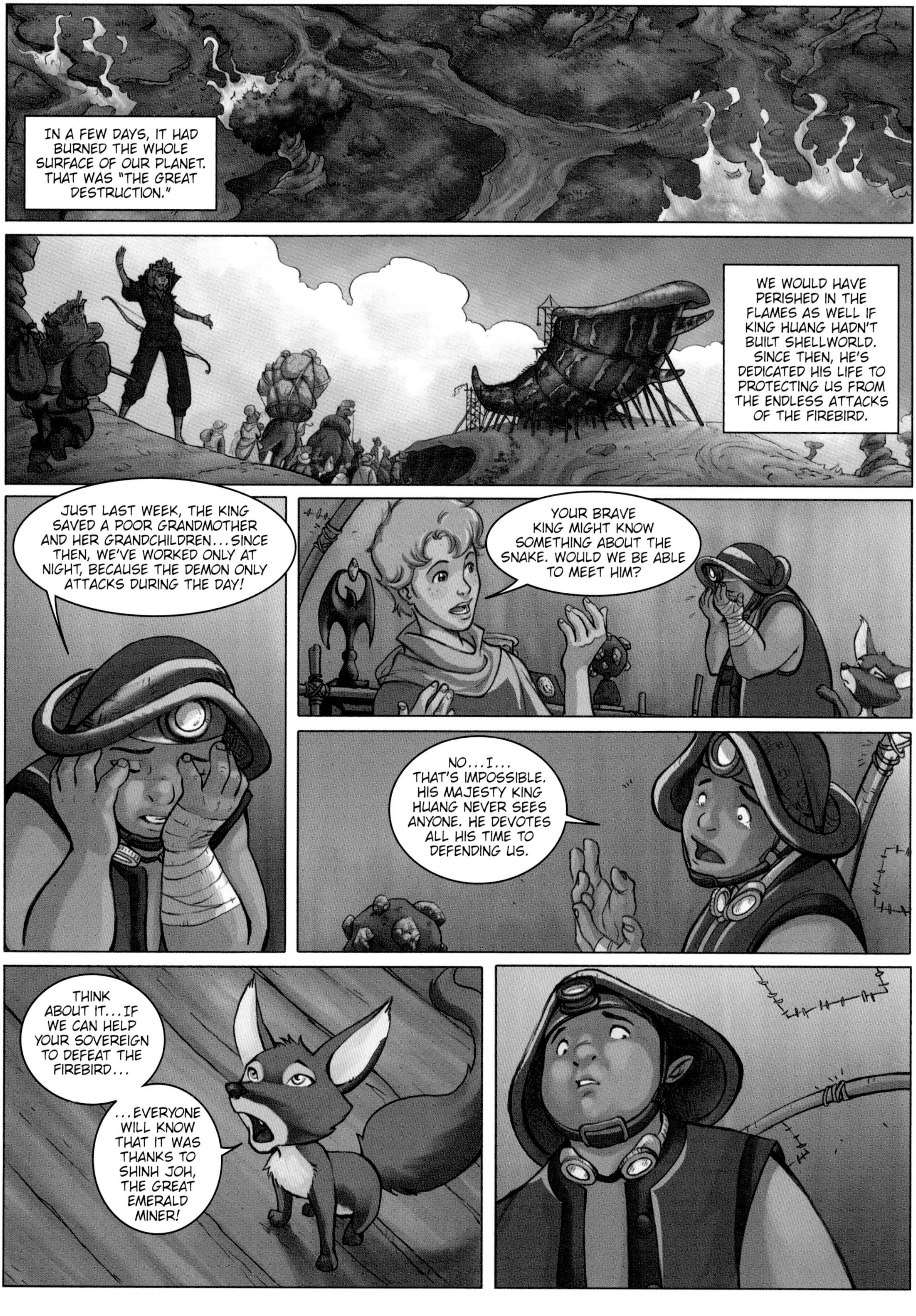
IN A FEW DAYS, IT HAD BURNED THE WHOLE SURFACE OF OUR PLANET. THAT WAS "THE GREAT DESTRUCTION."
WE WOULD HAVE PERISHED IN THE FLAMES AS WELL IF KING HUANG HADN'T BUILT SHELLWORLD. SINCE THEN, HE'S DEDICATED HIS LIFE TO PROTECTING US FROM THE ENDLESS ATTACKS OF THE FIREBIRD.
JUST LAST WEEK, THE KING SAVED A POOR GRANDMOTHER AND HER GRANDCHILDREN... SINCE THEN, WE'VE WORKED ONLY AT NIGHT, BECAUSE THE DEMON ONLY ATTACKS DURING THE DAY!
YOUR BRAVE KING MIGHT KNOW SOMETHING ABOUT THE SNAKE. WOULD WE BE ABLE TO MEET HIM?
NO... I... THAT'S IMPOSSIBLE. HIS MAJESTY KING HUANG NEVER SEES ANYONE. HE DEVOTES ALL HIS TIME TO DEFENDING US.
THINK ABOUT IT... IF WE CAN HELP YOUR SOVEREIGN TO DEFEAT THE FIREBIRD...
...EVERYONE WILL KNOW THAT IT WAS THANKS TO SHINH JOH, THE GREAT EMERALD MINER!

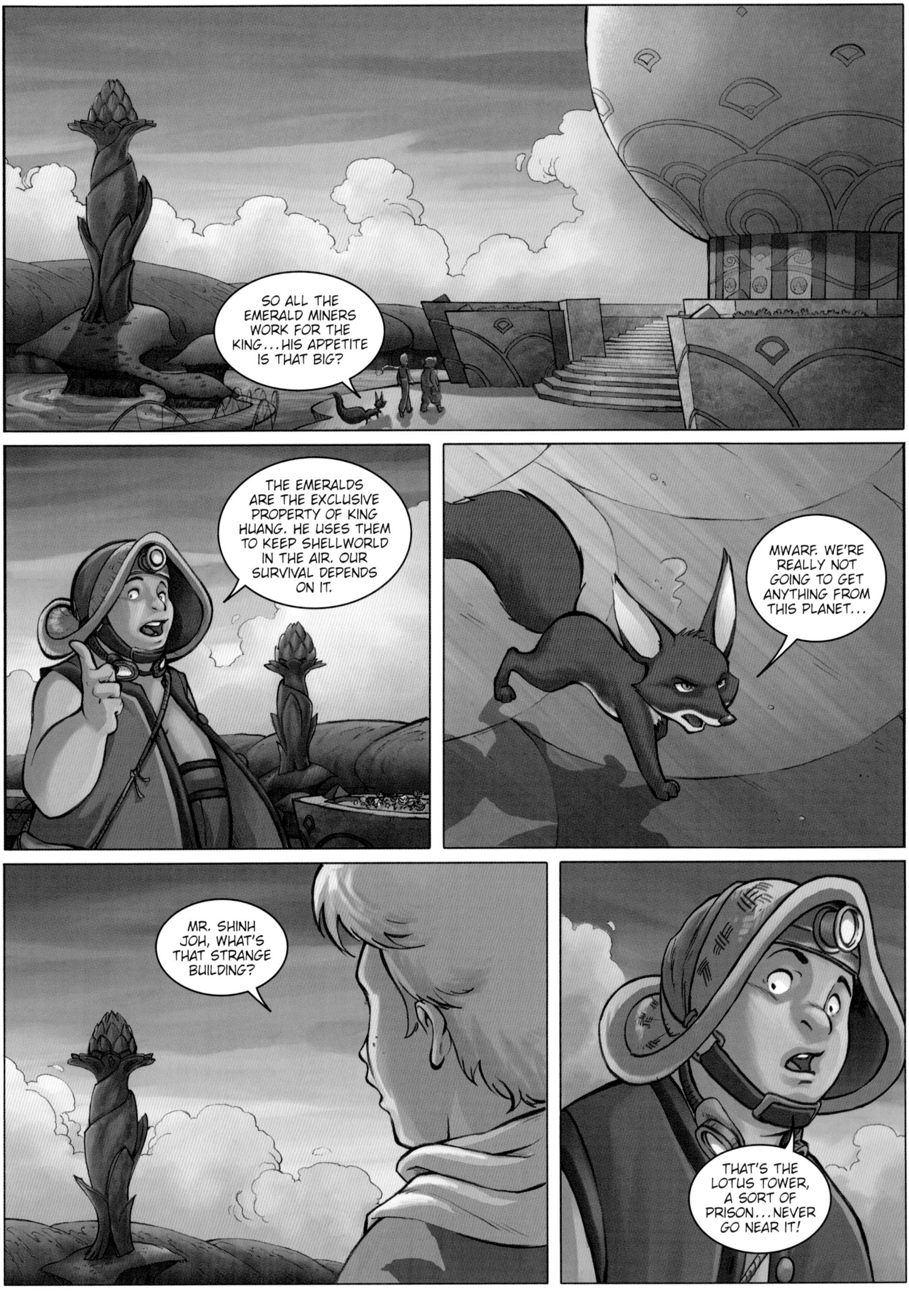
SO ALL THE EMERALD MINERS WORK FOR THE KING...HIS APPETITE IS THAT BIG?
THE EMERALDS ARE THE EXCLUSIVE PROPERTY OF KING HUANG. HE USES THEM TO KEEP SHELLWORLD IN THE AIR. OUR SURVIVAL DEPENDS ON IT.
MWARF. WE'RE REALLY NOT GOING TO GET ANYTHING FROM THIS PLANET...
MR. SHINH JOH, WHAT'S THAT STRANGE BUILDING?
THAT'S THE LOTUS TOWER, A SORT OF PRISON...NEVER GO NEAR IT!

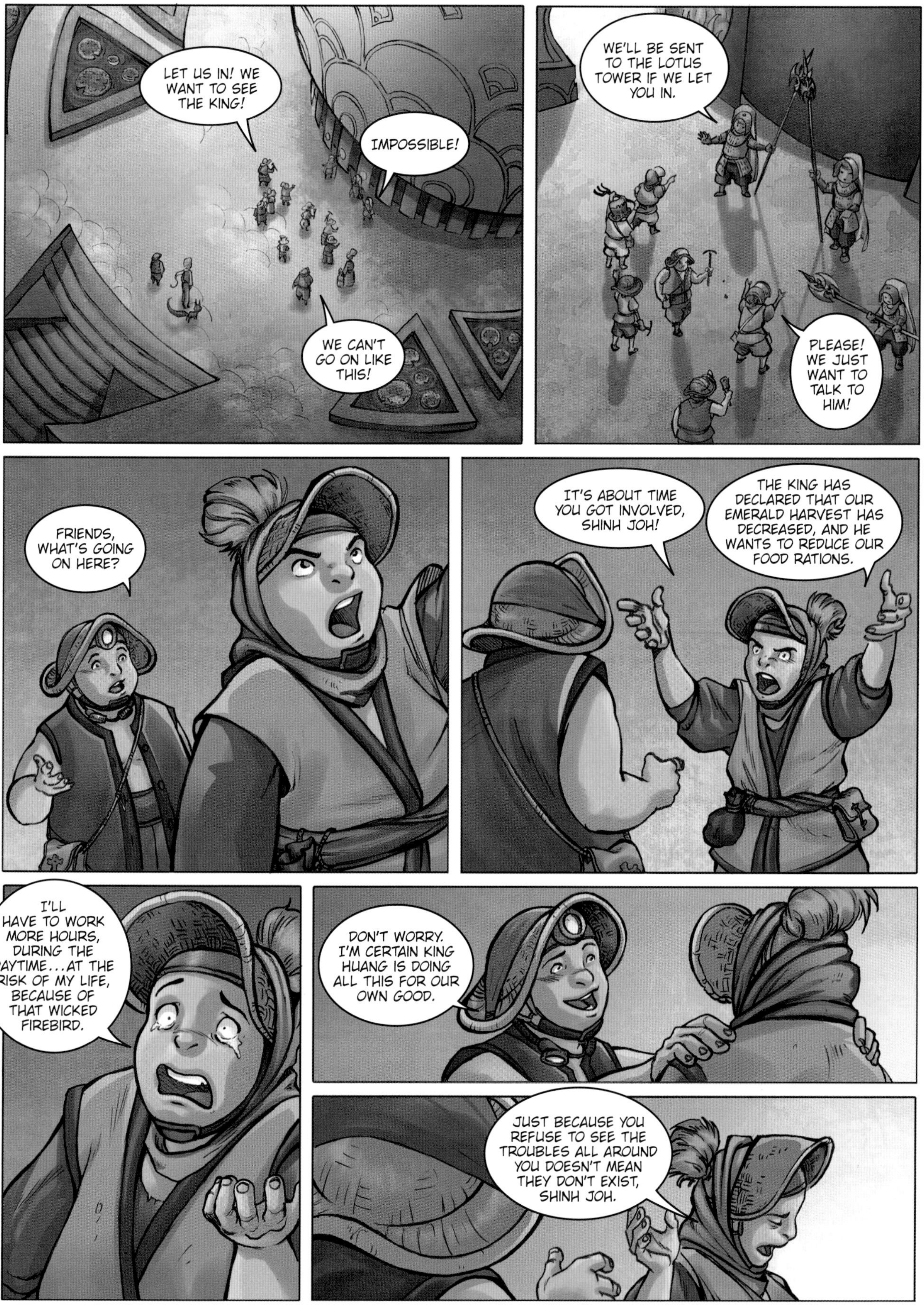
LET US IN! WE WANT TO SEE THE KING!
IMPOSSIBLE!
WE CAN'T GO ON LIKE THIS!
WE'LL BE SENT TO THE LOTUS TOWER IF WE LET YOU IN.
PLEASE! WE JUST WANT TO TALK TO HIM!
FRIENDS, WHAT'S GOING ON HERE?
IT'S ABOUT TIME YOU GOT INVOLVED, SHINH JOH!
THE KING HAS DECLARED THAT OUR EMERALD HARVEST HAS DECREASED, AND HE WANTS TO REDUCE OUR FOOD RATIONS.
I'LL HAVE TO WORK MORE HOURS, DURING THE DAYTIME...AT THE RISK OF MY LIFE, BECAUSE OF THAT WICKED FIREBIRD.
DON'T WORRY. I'M CERTAIN KING HUANG IS DOING ALL THIS FOR OUR OWN GOOD.
JUST BECAUSE YOU REFUSE TO SEE THE TROUBLES ALL AROUND YOU DOESN'T MEAN THEY DON'T EXIST, SHINH JOH.

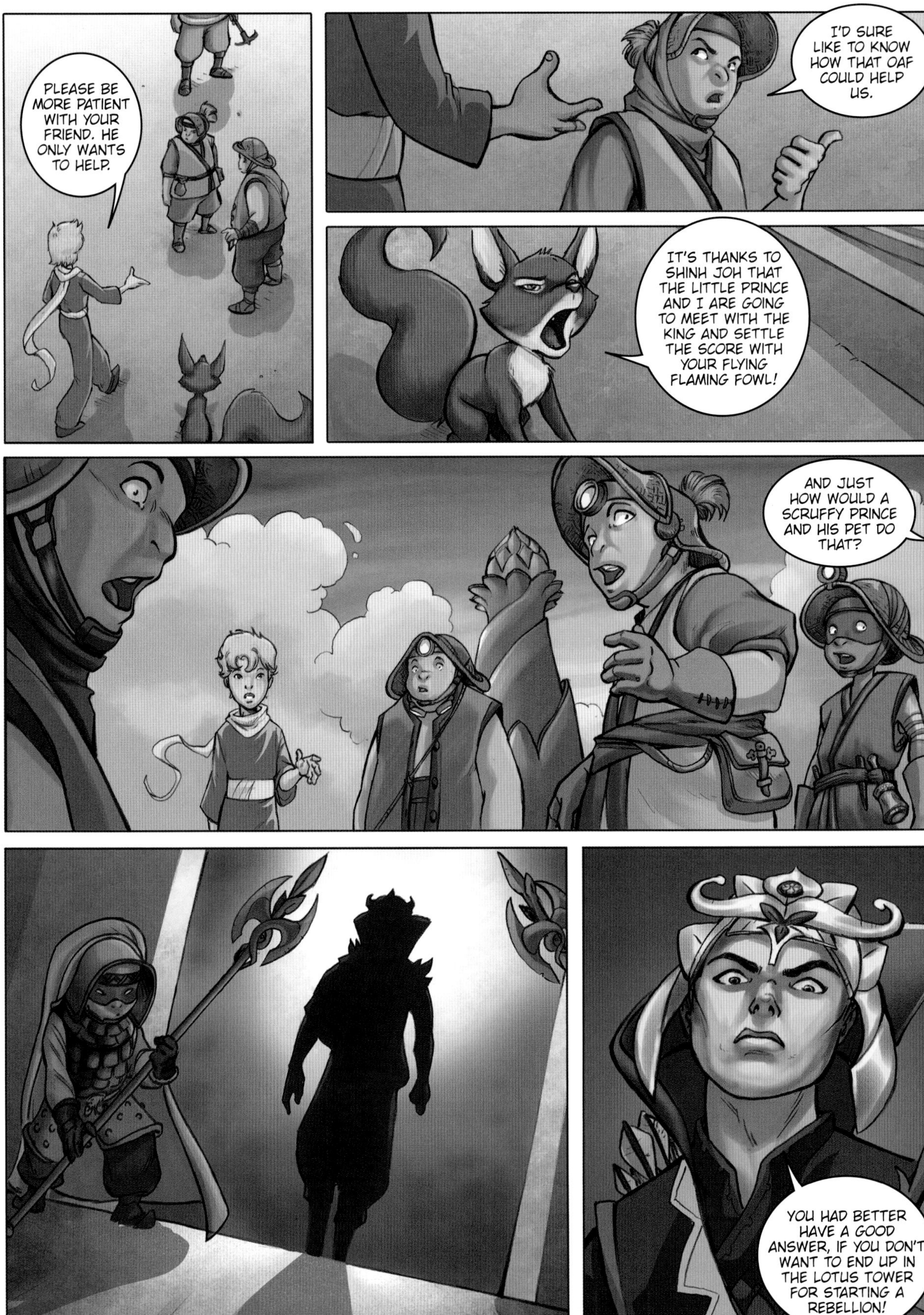
PLEASE BE MORE PATIENT WITH YOUR FRIEND. HE ONLY WANTS TO HELP.
I'D SURE LIKE TO KNOW HOW THAT OAF COULD HELP US.
IT'S THANKS TO SHINH JOH THAT THE LITTLE PRINCE AND I ARE GOING TO MEET WITH THE KING AND SETTLE THE SCORE WITH YOUR FLYING FLAMING FOWL!
AND JUST HOW WOULD A SCRUFFY PRINCE AND HIS PET DO THAT?
YOU HAD BETTER HAVE A GOOD ANSWER, IF YOU DON'T WANT TO END UP IN THE LOTUS TOWER FOR STARTING A REBELLION!

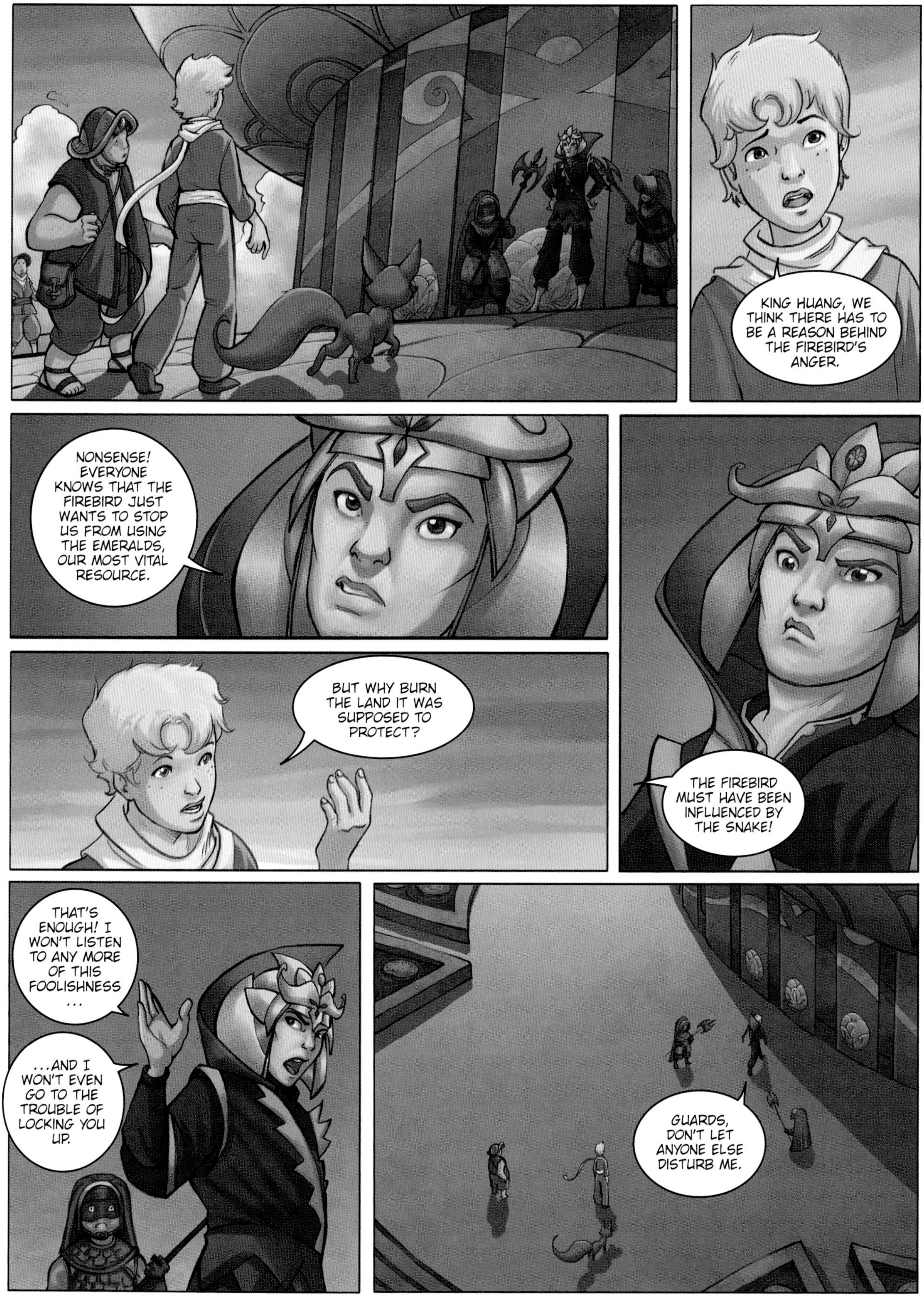
KING HUANG, WE THINK THERE HAS TO BE A REASON BEHIND THE FIREBIRD'S ANGER.
NONSENSE! EVERYONE KNOWS THAT THE FIREBIRD JUST WANTS TO STOP US FROM USING THE EMERALDS, OUR MOST VITAL RESOURCE.
BUT WHY BURN THE LAND IT WAS SUPPOSED TO PROTECT?
THE FIREBIRD MUST HAVE BEEN INFLUENCED BY THE SNAKE!
THAT'S ENOUGH! I WON'T LISTEN TO ANY MORE OF THIS FOOLISHNESS . . .
. . .AND I WON'T EVEN GO TO THE TROUBLE OF LOCKING YOU UP.
GUARDS, DON'T LET ANYONE ELSE DISTURB ME.

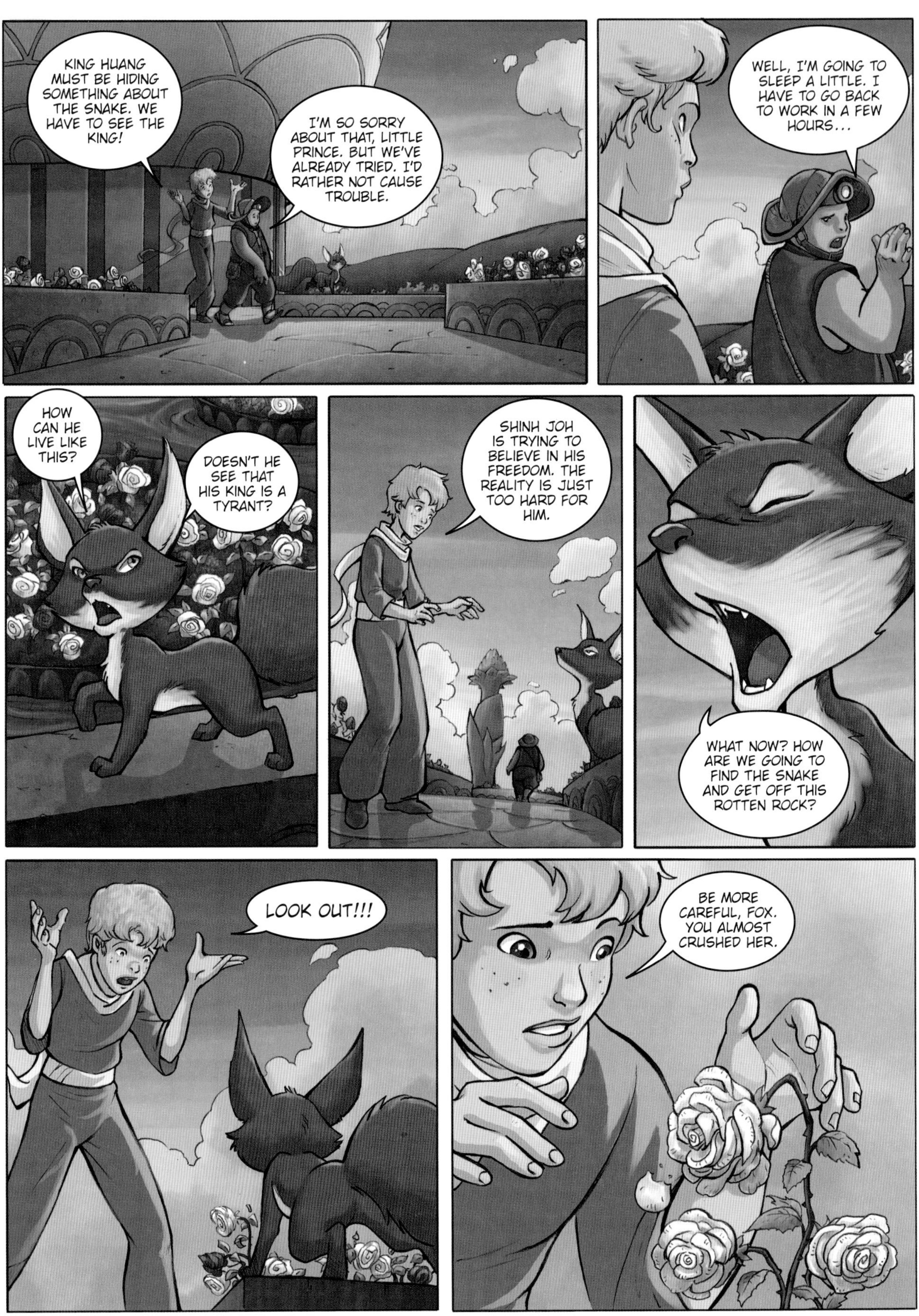
KING HUANG MUST BE HIDING SOMETHING ABOUT THE SNAKE. WE HAVE TO SEE THE KING!
I'M SO SORRY ABOUT THAT, LITTLE PRINCE. BUT WE'VE ALREADY TRIED. I'D RATHER NOT CAUSE TROUBLE.
WELL, I'M GOING TO SLEEP A LITTLE. I HAVE TO GO BACK TO WORK IN A FEW HOURS...
HOW CAN HE LIVE LIKE THIS?
DOESN'T HE SEE THAT HIS KING IS A TYRANT?
SHINH JOH IS TRYING TO BELIEVE IN HIS FREEDOM. THE REALITY IS JUST TOO HARD FOR HIM.
WHAT NOW? HOW ARE WE GOING TO FIND THE SNAKE AND GET OFF THIS ROTTEN ROCK?
LOOK OUT!!!
BE MORE CAREFUL, FOX. YOU ALMOST CRUSHED HER.

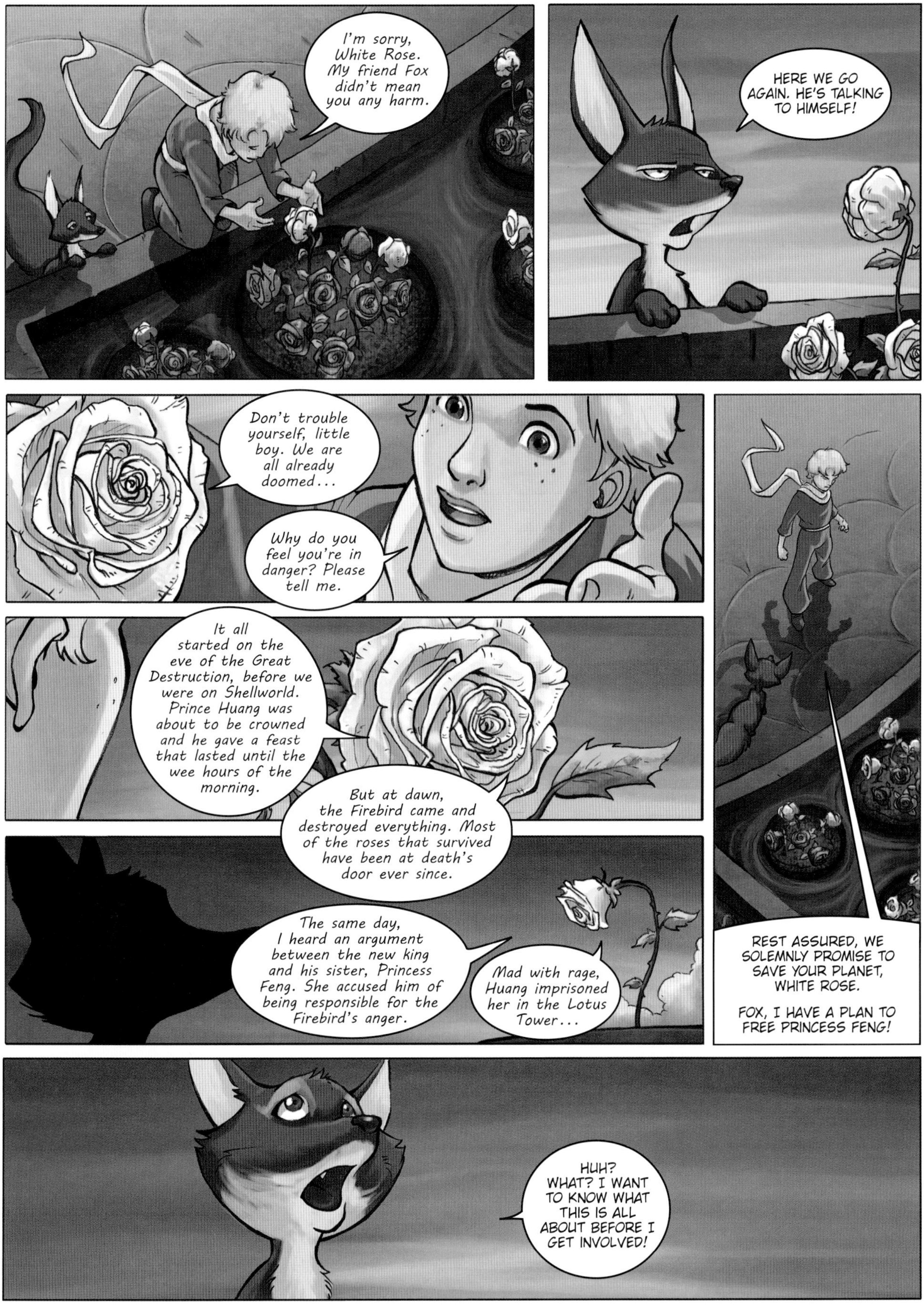
I'm sorry, White Rose. My friend Fox didn't mean you any harm.
HERE WE GO AGAIN. HE'S TALKING TO HIMSELF!
Don't trouble yourself, little boy. We are all already doomed...
Why do you feel you're in danger? Please tell me.
It all started on the eve of the Great Destruction, before we were on Shellworld. Prince Huang was about to be crowned and he gave a feast that lasted until the wee hours of the morning.
But at dawn, the Firebird came and destroyed everything. Most of the roses that survived have been at death's door ever since.
The same day, I heard an argument between the new king and his sister, Princess Feng. She accused him of being responsible for the Firebird's anger.
Mad with rage, Huang imprisoned her in the Lotus Tower...
REST ASSURED, WE SOLEMNLY PROMISE TO SAVE YOUR PLANET, WHITE ROSE.
FOX, I HAVE A PLAN TO FREE PRINCESS FENG!
HUH? WHAT? I WANT TO KNOW WHAT THIS IS ALL ABOUT BEFORE I GET INVOLVED!

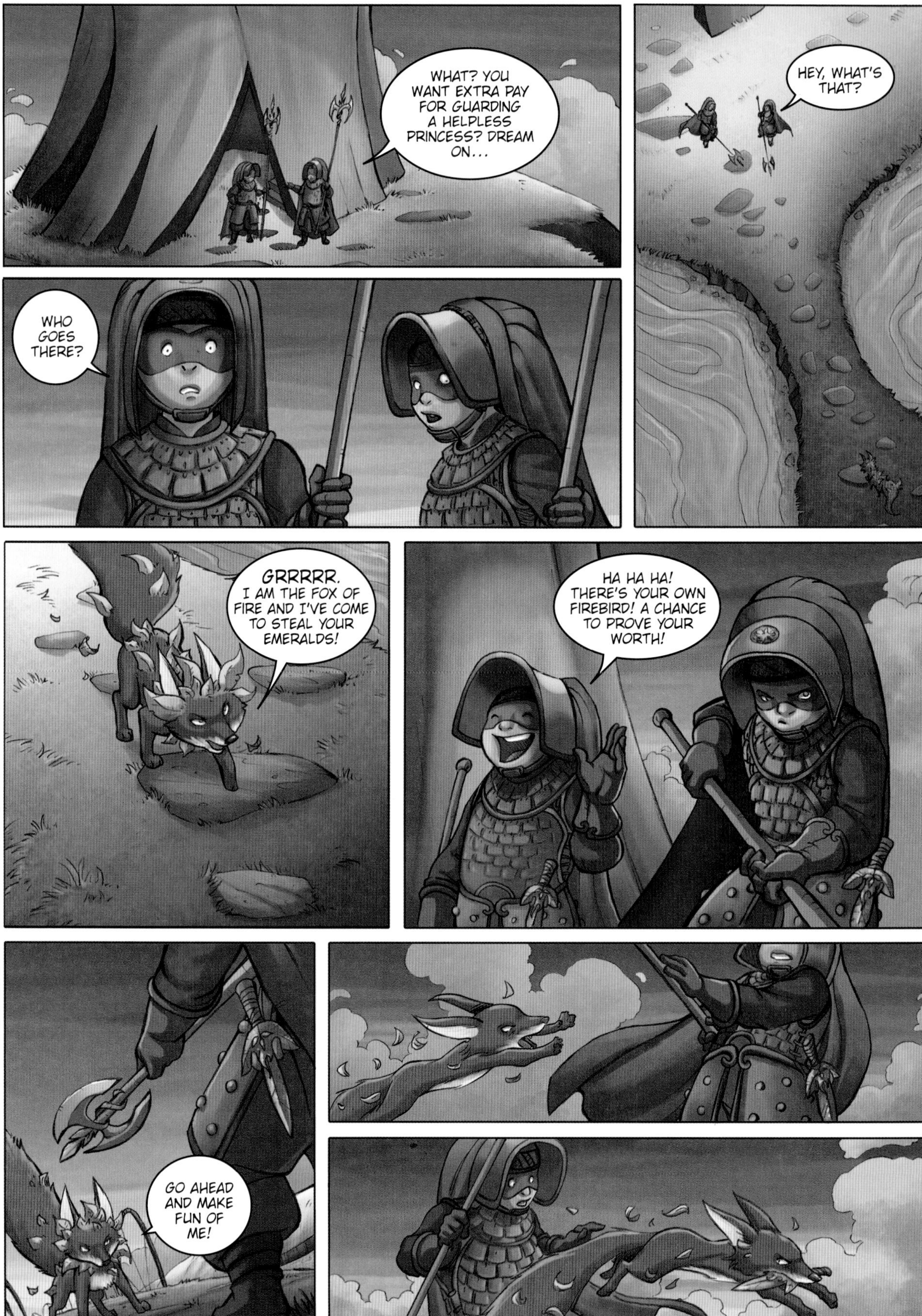
WHAT? YOU WANT EXTRA PAY FOR GUARDING A HELPLESS PRINCESS? DREAM ON...
HEY, WHAT'S THAT?
WHO GOES THERE?
GRRRRR. I AM THE FOX OF FIRE AND I'VE COME TO STEAL YOUR EMERALDS!
HA HA HA! THERE'S YOUR OWN FIREBIRD! A CHANCE TO PROVE YOUR WORTH!
GO AHEAD AND MAKE FUN OF ME!

STOP! THIEF!

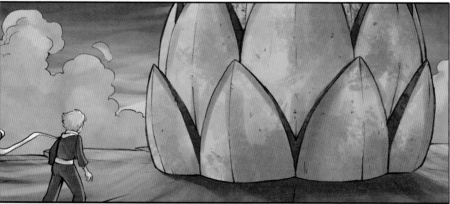

WHOOF! THOSE TWO WERE HARD TO SHAKE OFF!

THERE YOU GO. WHY DO YOU NEED THIS DAGGER? ISN'T YOUR PRINCELY SWORD ENOUGH FOR YOU?

I HAVE AN IDEA FOR GETTING INTO THE TOWER.

NOTHING CAN RESIST THESE EMERALDS!

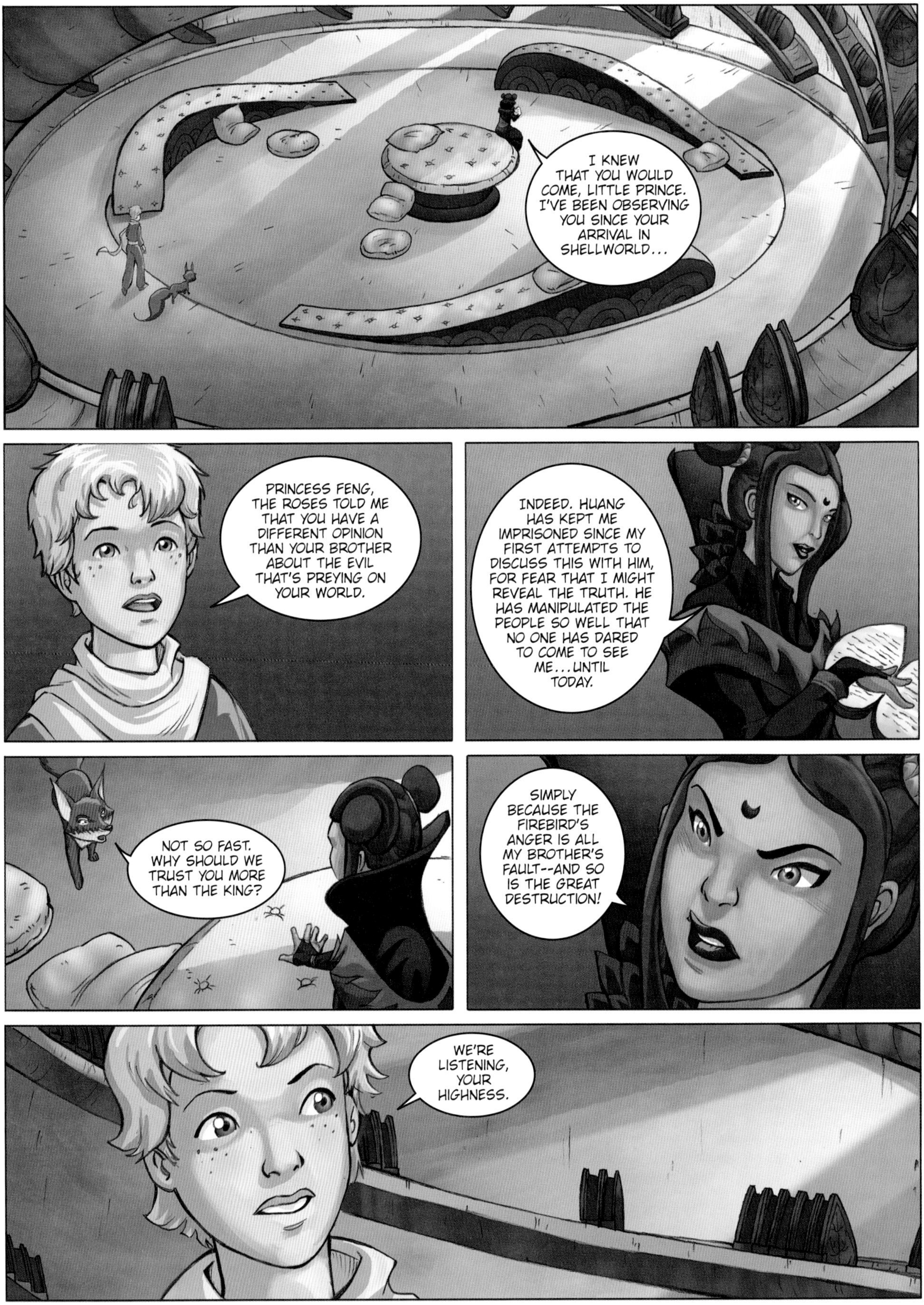
I KNEW THAT YOU WOULD COME, LITTLE PRINCE. I'VE BEEN OBSERVING YOU SINCE YOUR ARRIVAL IN SHELLWORLD...
PRINCESS FENG, THE ROSES TOLD ME THAT YOU HAVE A DIFFERENT OPINION THAN YOUR BROTHER ABOUT THE EVIL THAT'S PREYING ON YOUR WORLD.
INDEED. HUANG HAS KEPT ME IMPRISONED SINCE MY FIRST ATTEMPTS TO DISCUSS THIS WITH HIM, FOR FEAR THAT I MIGHT REVEAL THE TRUTH. HE HAS MANIPULATED THE PEOPLE SO WELL THAT NO ONE HAS DARED TO COME TO SEE ME...UNTIL TODAY.
NOT SO FAST. WHY SHOULD WE TRUST YOU MORE THAN THE KING?
SIMPLY BECAUSE THE FIREBIRD'S ANGER IS ALL MY BROTHER'S FAULT--AND SO IS THE GREAT DESTRUCTION!
WE'RE LISTENING, YOUR HIGHNESS.

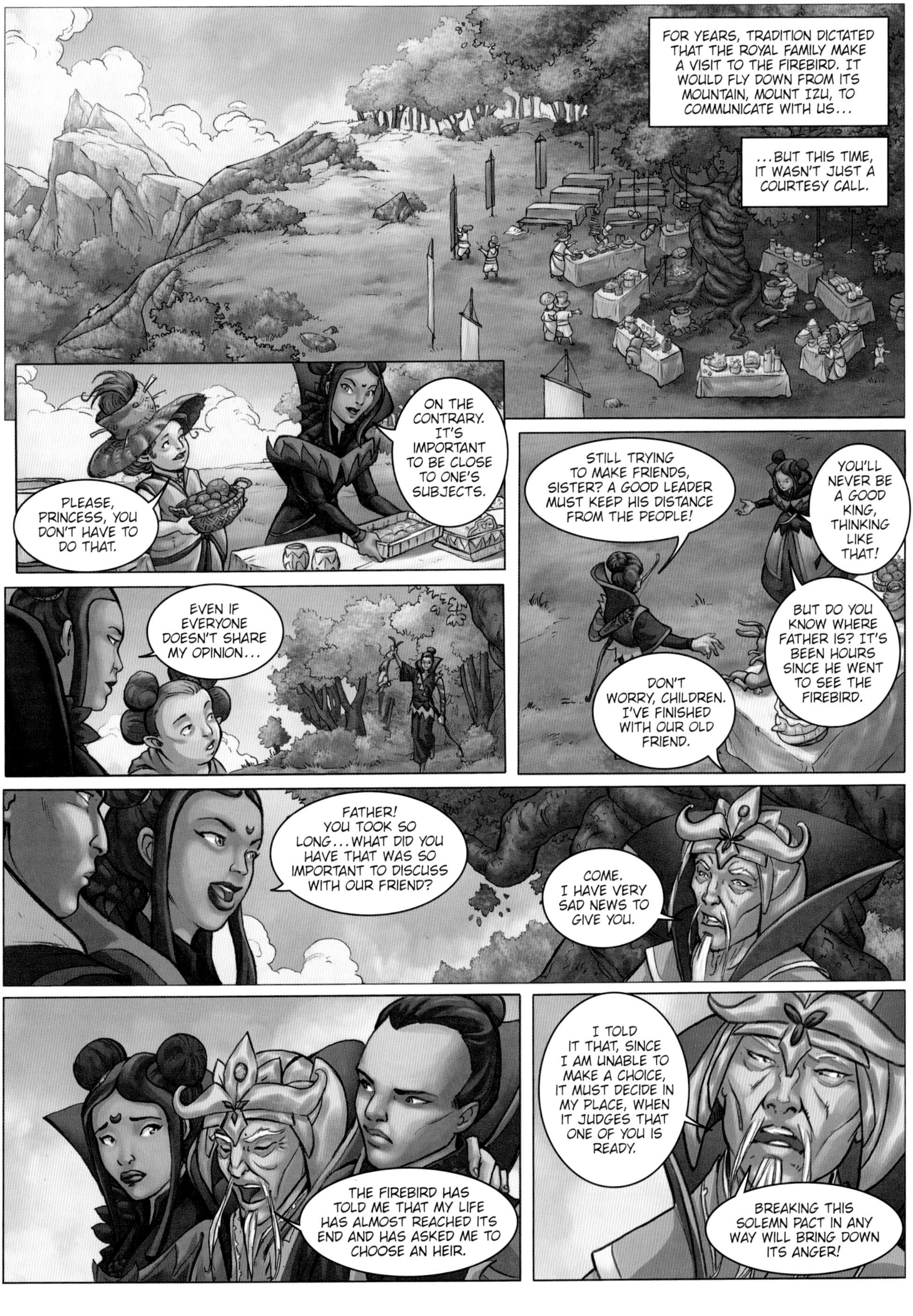
FOR YEARS, TRADITION DICTATED THAT THE ROYAL FAMILY MAKE A VISIT TO THE FIREBIRD. IT WOULD FLY DOWN FROM ITS MOUNTAIN, MOUNT IZU, TO COMMUNICATE WITH US...
...BUT THIS TIME, IT WASN'T JUST A COURTESY CALL.
PLEASE, PRINCESS, YOU DON'T HAVE TO DO THAT.
ON THE CONTRARY. IT'S IMPORTANT TO BE CLOSE TO ONE'S SUBJECTS.
EVEN IF EVERYONE DOESN'T SHARE MY OPINION...
STILL TRYING TO MAKE FRIENDS, SISTER? A GOOD LEADER MUST KEEP HIS DISTANCE FROM THE PEOPLE!
YOU'LL NEVER BE A GOOD KING, THINKING LIKE THAT!
BUT DO YOU KNOW WHERE FATHER IS? IT'S BEEN HOURS SINCE HE WENT TO SEE THE FIREBIRD.
DON'T WORRY, CHILDREN. I'VE FINISHED WITH OUR OLD FRIEND.
FATHER! YOU TOOK SO LONG... WHAT DID YOU HAVE THAT WAS SO IMPORTANT TO DISCUSS WITH OUR FRIEND?
COME. I HAVE VERY SAD NEWS TO GIVE YOU.
THE FIREBIRD HAS TOLD ME THAT MY LIFE HAS ALMOST REACHED ITS END AND HAS ASKED ME TO CHOOSE AN HEIR.
I TOLD IT THAT, SINCE I AM UNABLE TO MAKE A CHOICE, IT MUST DECIDE IN MY PLACE, WHEN IT JUDGES THAT ONE OF YOU IS READY.
BREAKING THIS SOLEMN PACT IN ANY WAY WILL BRING DOWN ITS ANGER!

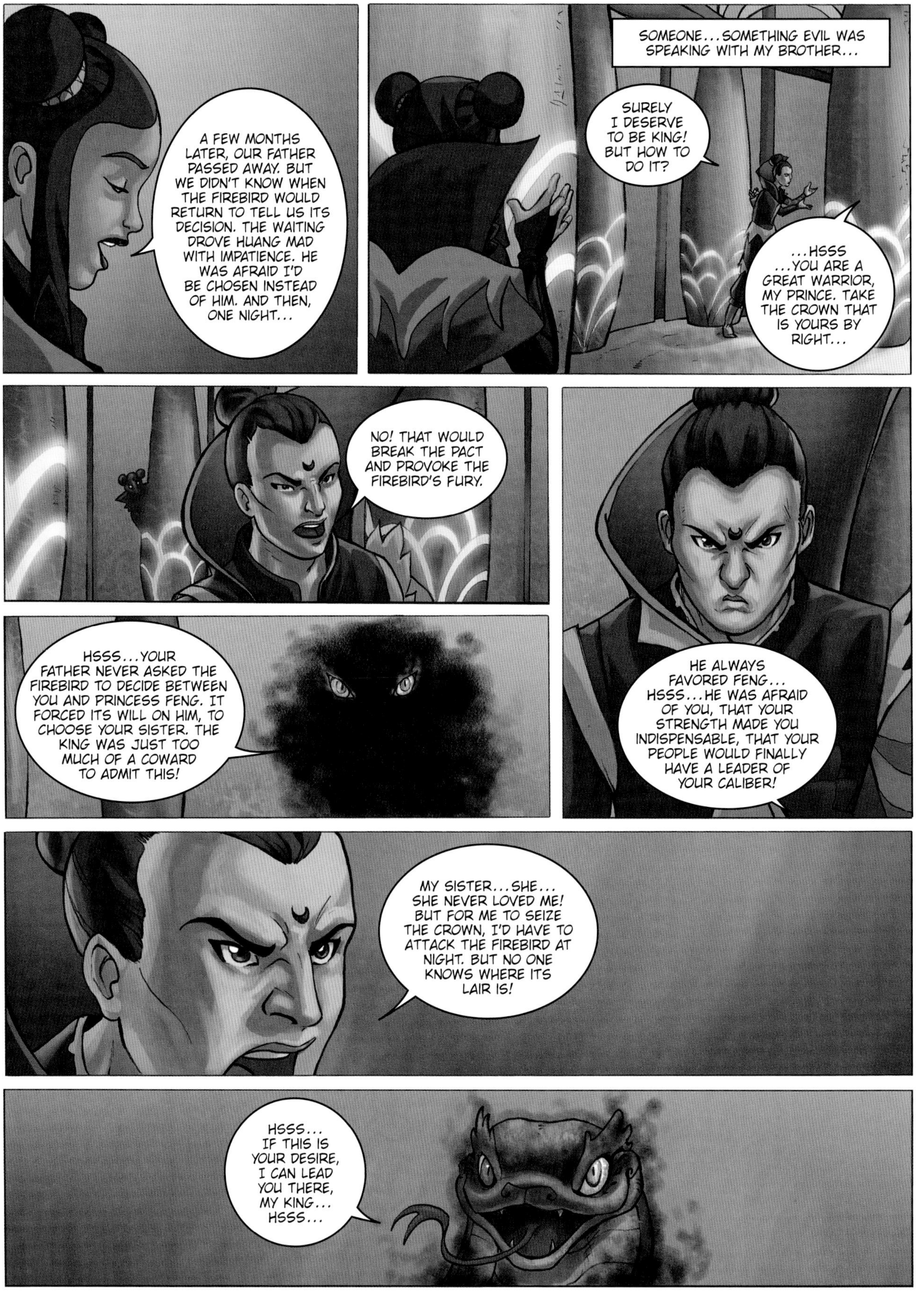
A FEW MONTHS LATER, OUR FATHER PASSED AWAY. BUT WE DIDN'T KNOW WHEN THE FIREBIRD WOULD RETURN TO TELL US ITS DECISION. THE WAITING DROVE HUANG MAD WITH IMPATIENCE. HE WAS AFRAID I'D BE CHOSEN INSTEAD OF HIM. AND THEN, ONE NIGHT...
SOMEONE...SOMETHING EVIL WAS SPEAKING WITH MY BROTHER...
SURELY I DESERVE TO BE KING! BUT HOW TO DO IT?
...HSSS ...YOU ARE A GREAT WARRIOR, MY PRINCE. TAKE THE CROWN THAT IS YOURS BY RIGHT...
NO! THAT WOULD BREAK THE PACT AND PROVOKE THE FIREBIRD'S FURY.
HSSS...YOUR FATHER NEVER ASKED THE FIREBIRD TO DECIDE BETWEEN YOU AND PRINCESS FENG. IT FORCED ITS WILL ON HIM, TO CHOOSE YOUR SISTER. THE KING WAS JUST TOO MUCH OF A COWARD TO ADMIT THIS!
HE ALWAYS FAVORED FENG... HSSS...HE WAS AFRAID OF YOU, THAT YOUR STRENGTH MADE YOU INDISPENSABLE, THAT YOUR PEOPLE WOULD FINALLY HAVE A LEADER OF YOUR CALIBER!
MY SISTER...SHE... SHE NEVER LOVED ME! BUT FOR ME TO SEIZE THE CROWN, I'D HAVE TO ATTACK THE FIREBIRD AT NIGHT. BUT NO ONE KNOWS WHERE ITS LAIR IS!
HSSS... IF THIS IS YOUR DESIRE, I CAN LEAD YOU THERE, MY KING... HSSS...

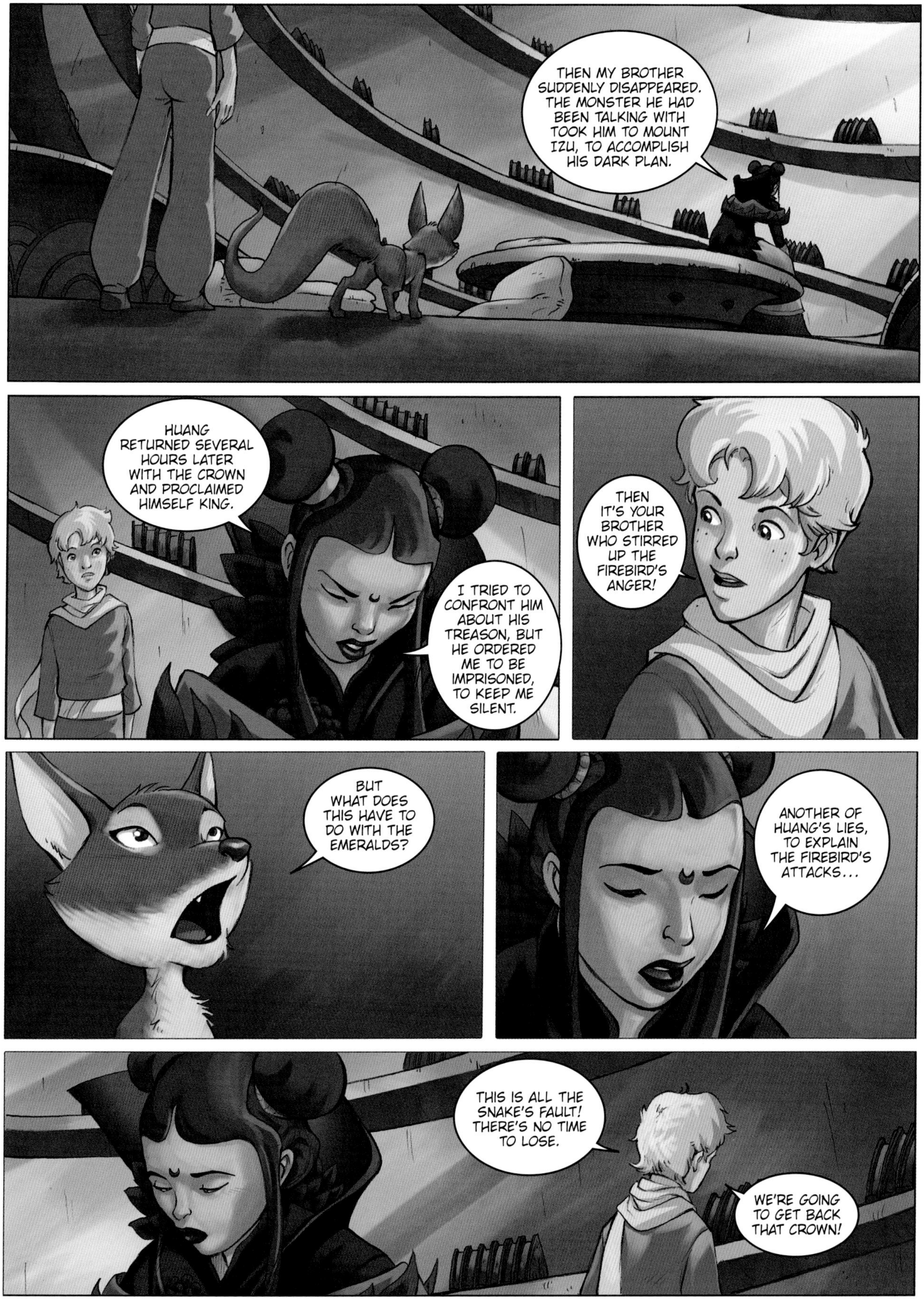
THEN MY BROTHER SUDDENLY DISAPPEARED. THE MONSTER HE HAD BEEN TALKING WITH TOOK HIM TO MOUNT IZU, TO ACCOMPLISH HIS DARK PLAN.
HUANG RETURNED SEVERAL HOURS LATER WITH THE CROWN AND PROCLAIMED HIMSELF KING.
I TRIED TO CONFRONT HIM ABOUT HIS TREASON, BUT HE ORDERED ME TO BE IMPRISONED, TO KEEP ME SILENT.
THEN IT'S YOUR BROTHER WHO STIRRED UP THE FIREBIRD'S ANGER!
BUT WHAT DOES THIS HAVE TO DO WITH THE EMERALDS?
ANOTHER OF HUANG'S LIES, TO EXPLAIN THE FIREBIRD'S ATTACKS...
THIS IS ALL THE SNAKE'S FAULT! THERE'S NO TIME TO LOSE.
WE'RE GOING TO GET BACK THAT CROWN!

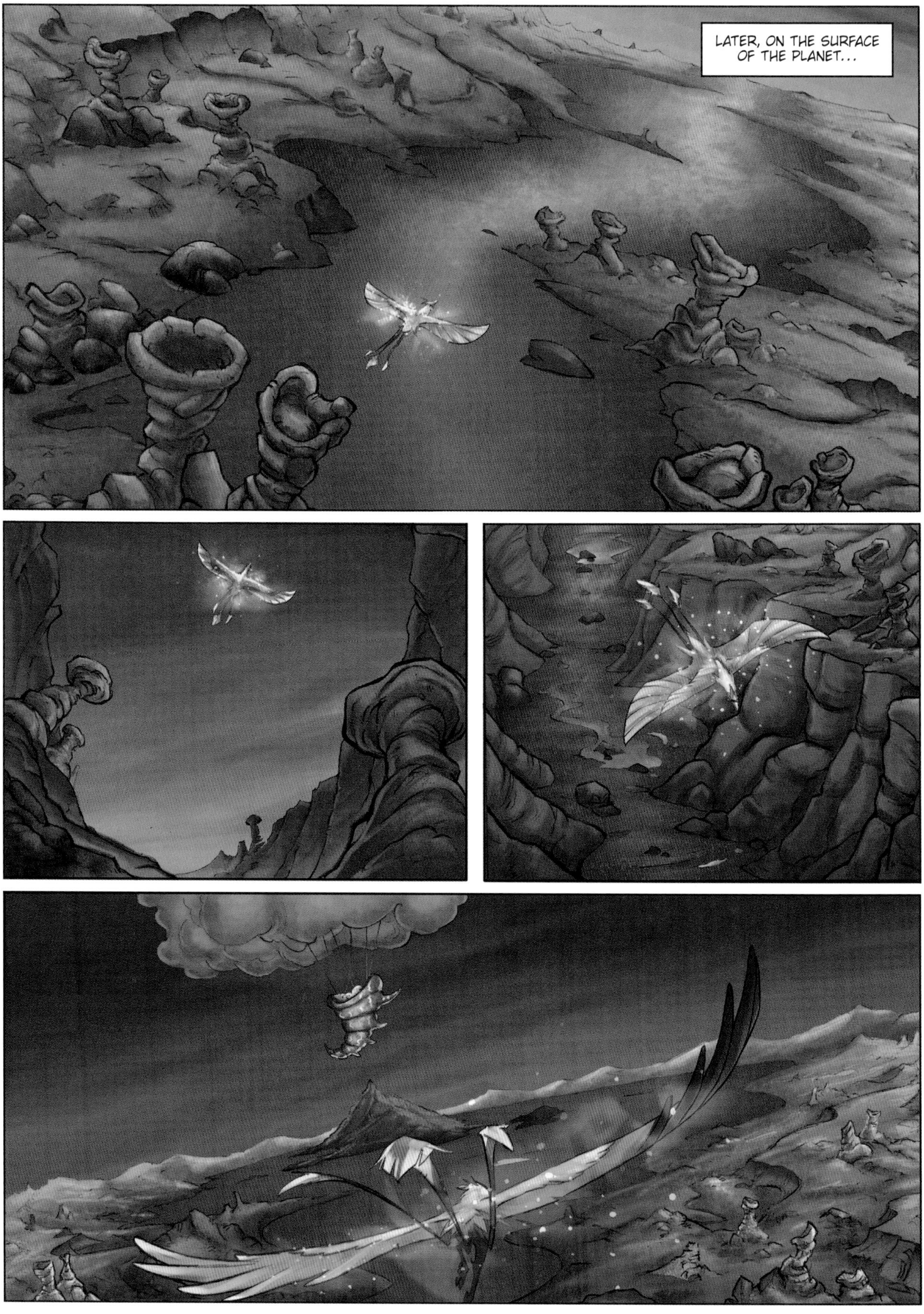
LATER, ON THE SURFACE OF THE PLANET...

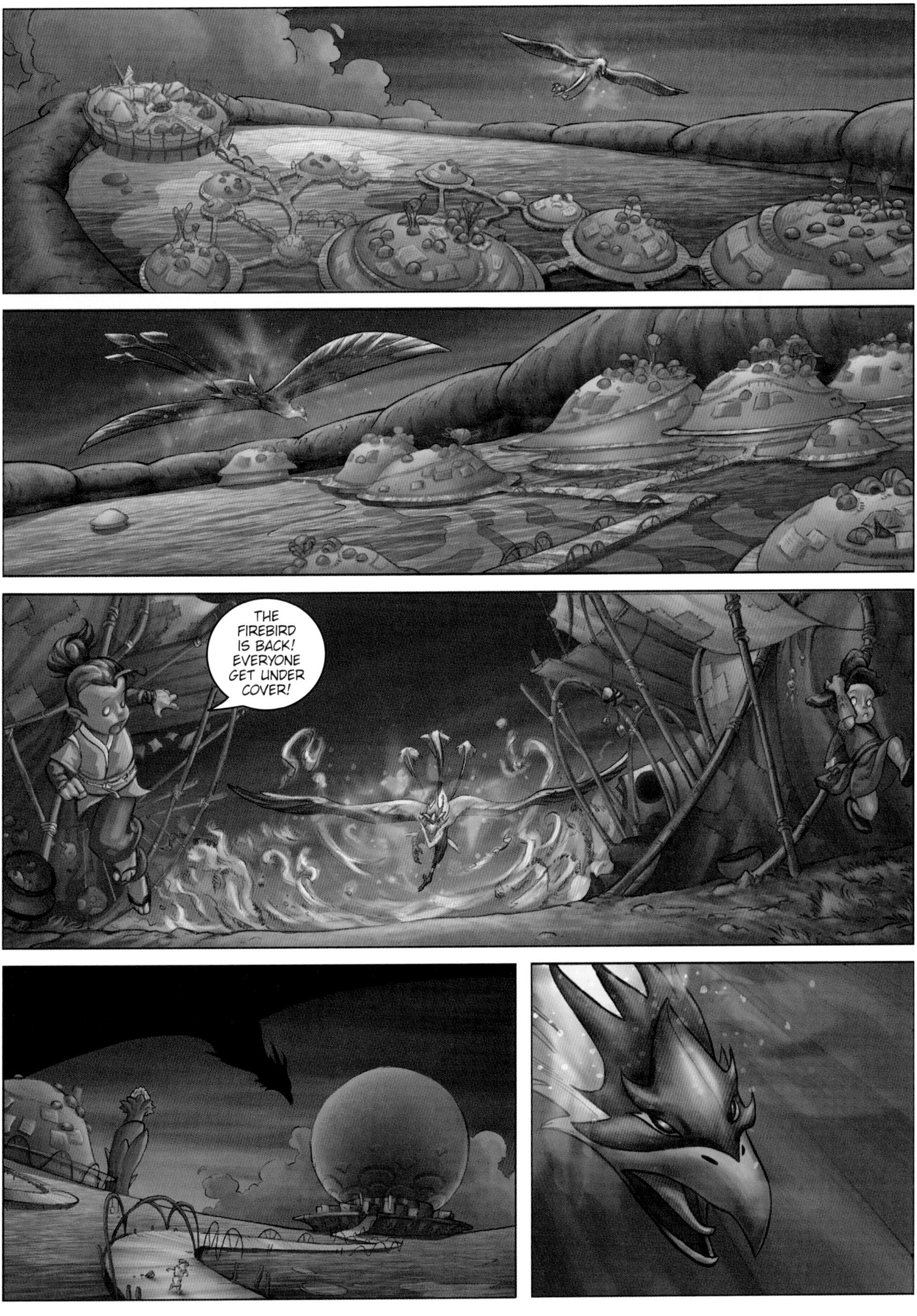
THE FIREBIRD IS BACK! EVERYONE GET UNDER COVER!

COME, BIRD OF
ILL OMEN!

DIE!

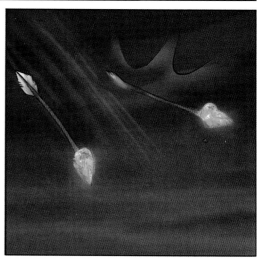

JUST IN TIME!

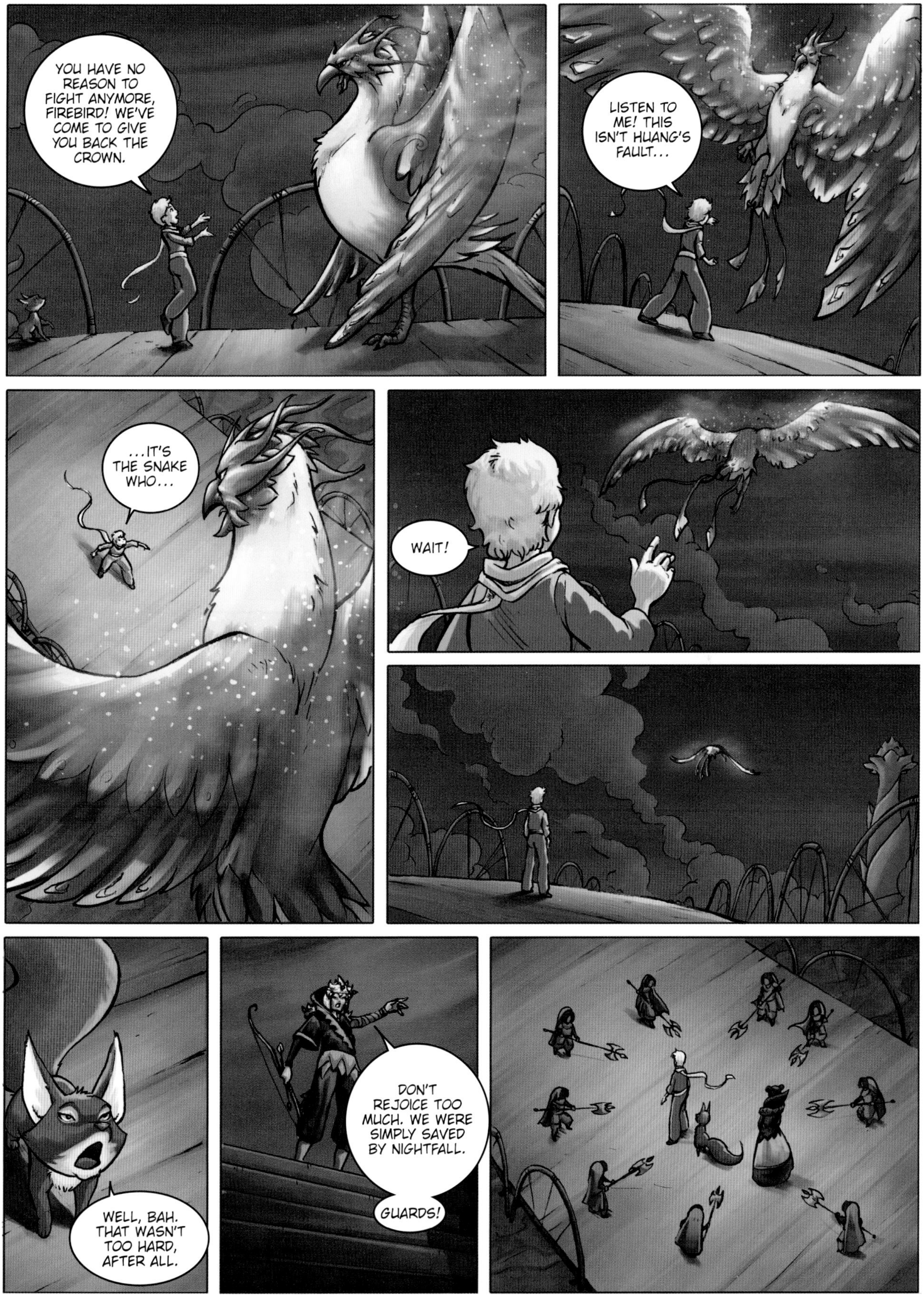
YOU HAVE NO REASON TO FIGHT ANYMORE, FIREBIRD! WE'VE COME TO GIVE YOU BACK THE CROWN.
LISTEN TO ME! THIS ISN'T HUANG'S FAULT...
...IT'S THE SNAKE WHO...
WAIT!
WELL, BAH. THAT WASN'T TOO HARD, AFTER ALL.
DON'T REJOICE TOO MUCH. WE WERE SIMPLY SAVED BY NIGHTFALL.
GUARDS!

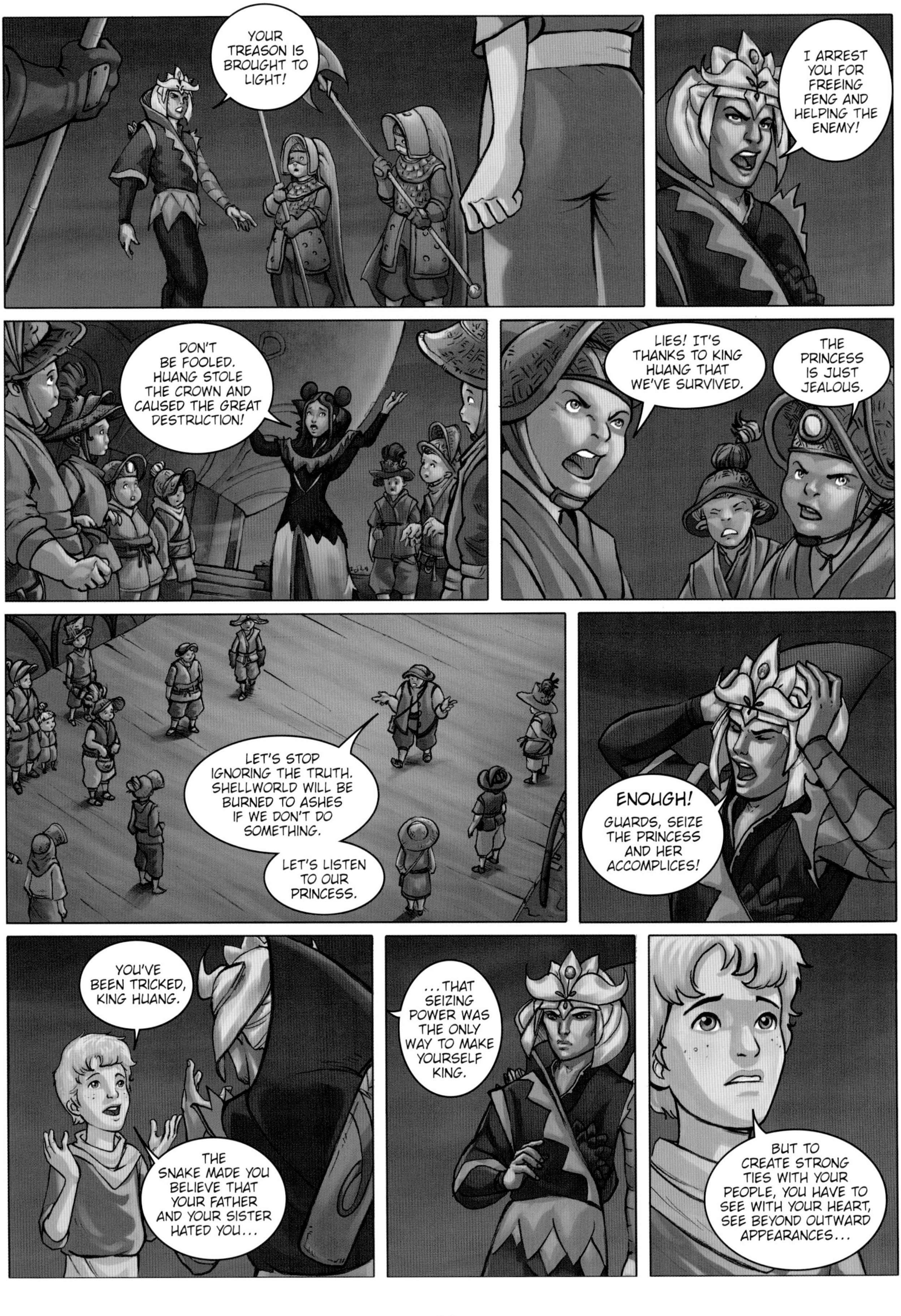
YOUR TREASON IS BROUGHT TO LIGHT!
I ARREST YOU FOR FREEING FENG AND HELPING THE ENEMY!
DON'T BE FOOLED. HUANG STOLE THE CROWN AND CAUSED THE GREAT DESTRUCTION!
LIES! IT'S THANKS TO KING HUANG THAT WE'VE SURVIVED.
THE PRINCESS IS JUST JEALOUS.
LET'S STOP IGNORING THE TRUTH. SHELLWORLD WILL BE BURNED TO ASHES IF WE DON'T DO SOMETHING.
LET'S LISTEN TO OUR PRINCESS.
ENOUGH! GUARDS, SEIZE THE PRINCESS AND HER ACCOMPLICES!
YOU'VE BEEN TRICKED, KING HUANG.
THE SNAKE MADE YOU BELIEVE THAT YOUR FATHER AND YOUR SISTER HATED YOU...
...THAT SEIZING POWER WAS THE ONLY WAY TO MAKE YOURSELF KING.
BUT TO CREATE STRONG TIES WITH YOUR PEOPLE, YOU HAVE TO SEE WITH YOUR HEART, SEE BEYOND OUTWARD APPEARANCES...

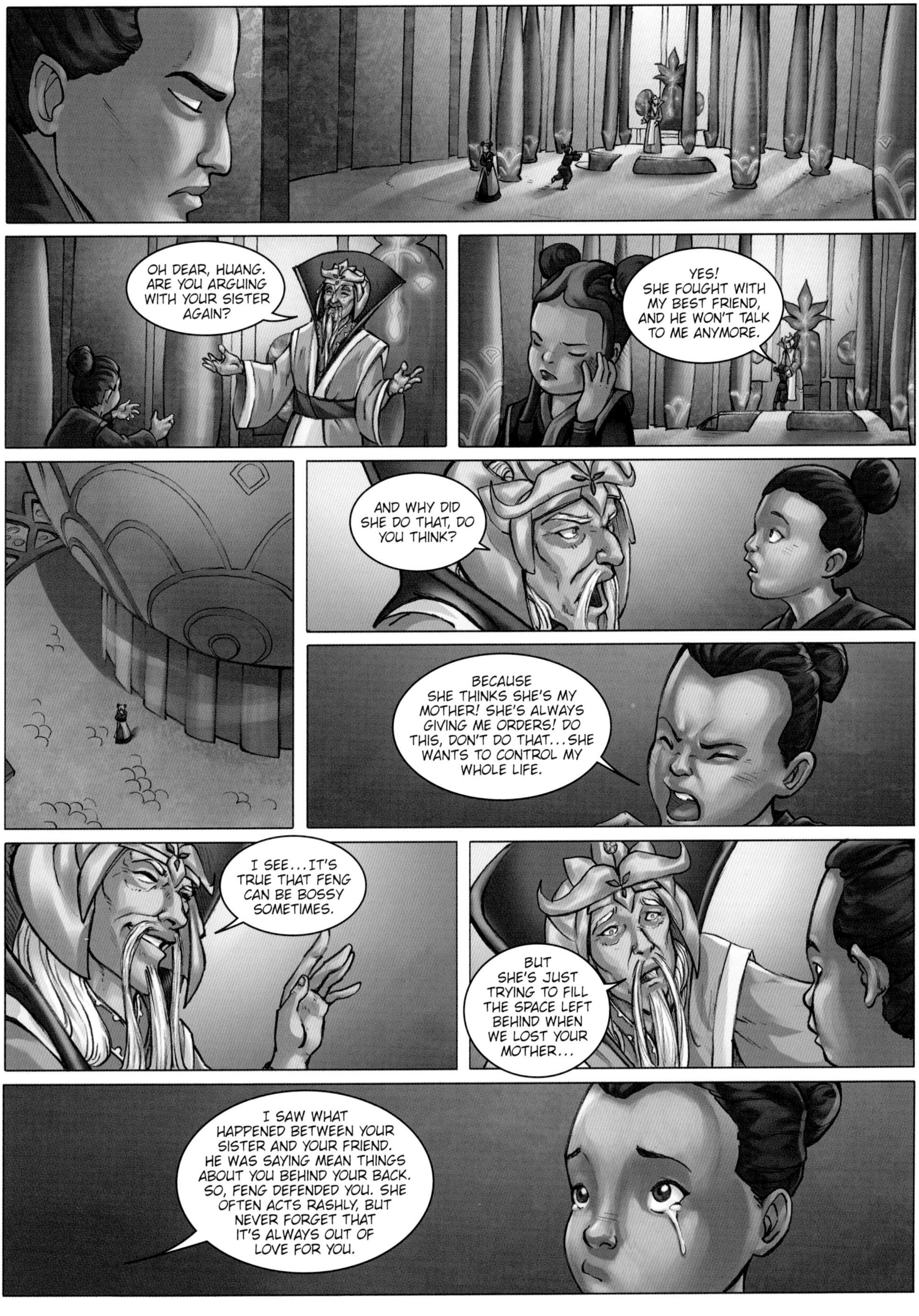
OH DEAR, HUANG. ARE YOU ARGUING WITH YOUR SISTER AGAIN?
YES! SHE FOUGHT WITH MY BEST FRIEND, AND HE WON'T TALK TO ME ANYMORE.
AND WHY DID SHE DO THAT, DO YOU THINK?
BECAUSE SHE THINKS SHE'S MY MOTHER! SHE'S ALWAYS GIVING ME ORDERS! DO THIS, DON'T DO THAT... SHE WANTS TO CONTROL MY WHOLE LIFE.
I SEE... IT'S TRUE THAT FENG CAN BE BOSSY SOMETIMES.
BUT SHE'S JUST TRYING TO FILL THE SPACE LEFT BEHIND WHEN WE LOST YOUR MOTHER...
I SAW WHAT HAPPENED BETWEEN YOUR SISTER AND YOUR FRIEND. HE WAS SAYING MEAN THINGS ABOUT YOU BEHIND YOUR BACK. SO, FENG DEFENDED YOU. SHE OFTEN ACTS RASHLY, BUT NEVER FORGET THAT IT'S ALWAYS OUT OF LOVE FOR YOU.

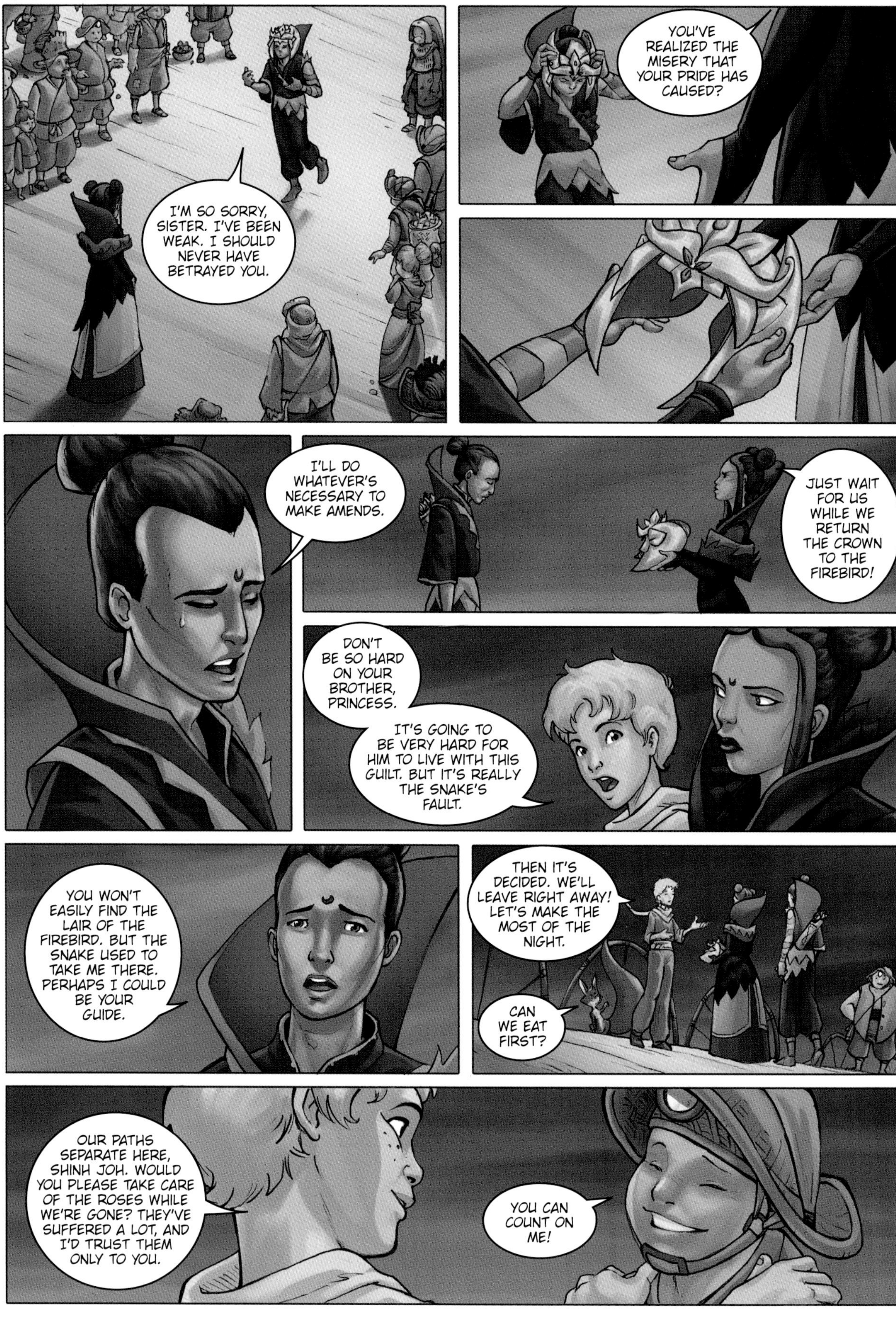
I'M SO SORRY, SISTER. I'VE BEEN WEAK. I SHOULD NEVER HAVE BETRAYED YOU.
YOU'VE REALIZED THE MISERY THAT YOUR PRIDE HAS CAUSED?
I'LL DO WHATEVER'S NECESSARY TO MAKE AMENDS.
JUST WAIT FOR US WHILE WE RETURN THE CROWN TO THE FIREBIRD!
DON'T BE SO HARD ON YOUR BROTHER, PRINCESS.
IT'S GOING TO BE VERY HARD FOR HIM TO LIVE WITH THIS GUILT. BUT IT'S REALLY THE SNAKE'S FAULT.
YOU WON'T EASILY FIND THE LAIR OF THE FIREBIRD. BUT THE SNAKE USED TO TAKE ME THERE. PERHAPS I COULD BE YOUR GUIDE.
THEN IT'S DECIDED. WE'LL LEAVE RIGHT AWAY! LET'S MAKE THE MOST OF THE NIGHT.
CAN WE EAT FIRST?
OUR PATHS SEPARATE HERE, SHINH JOH. WOULD YOU PLEASE TAKE CARE OF THE ROSES WHILE WE'RE GONE? THEY'VE SUFFERED A LOT, AND I'D TRUST THEM ONLY TO YOU.
YOU CAN COUNT ON ME!

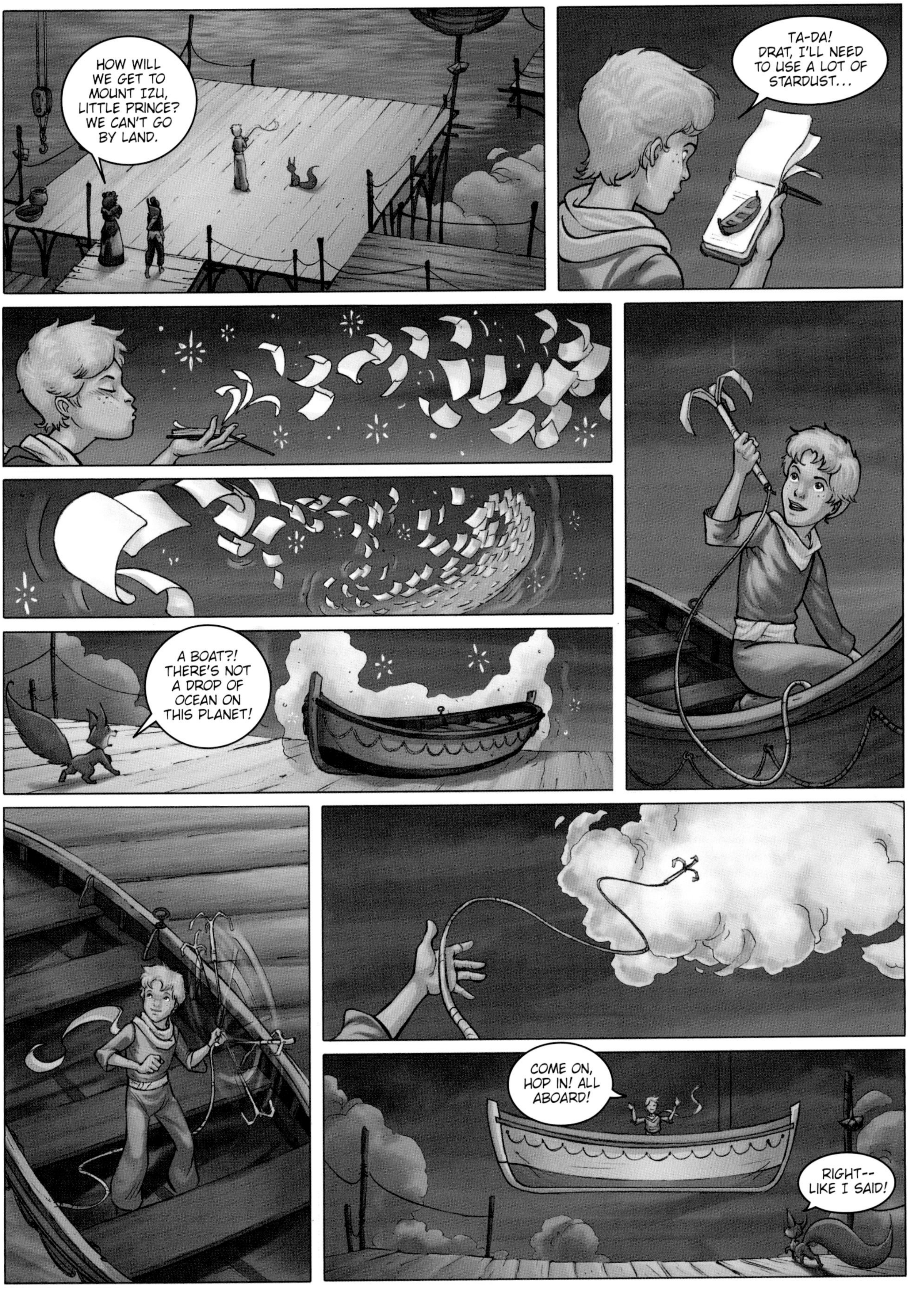
HOW WILL WE GET TO MOUNT IZU, LITTLE PRINCE? WE CAN'T GO BY LAND.
TA-DA! DRAT, I'LL NEED TO USE A LOT OF STARDUST...
A BOAT?! THERE'S NOT A DROP OF OCEAN ON THIS PLANET!
COME ON, HOP IN! ALL ABOARD!
RIGHT-- LIKE I SAID!

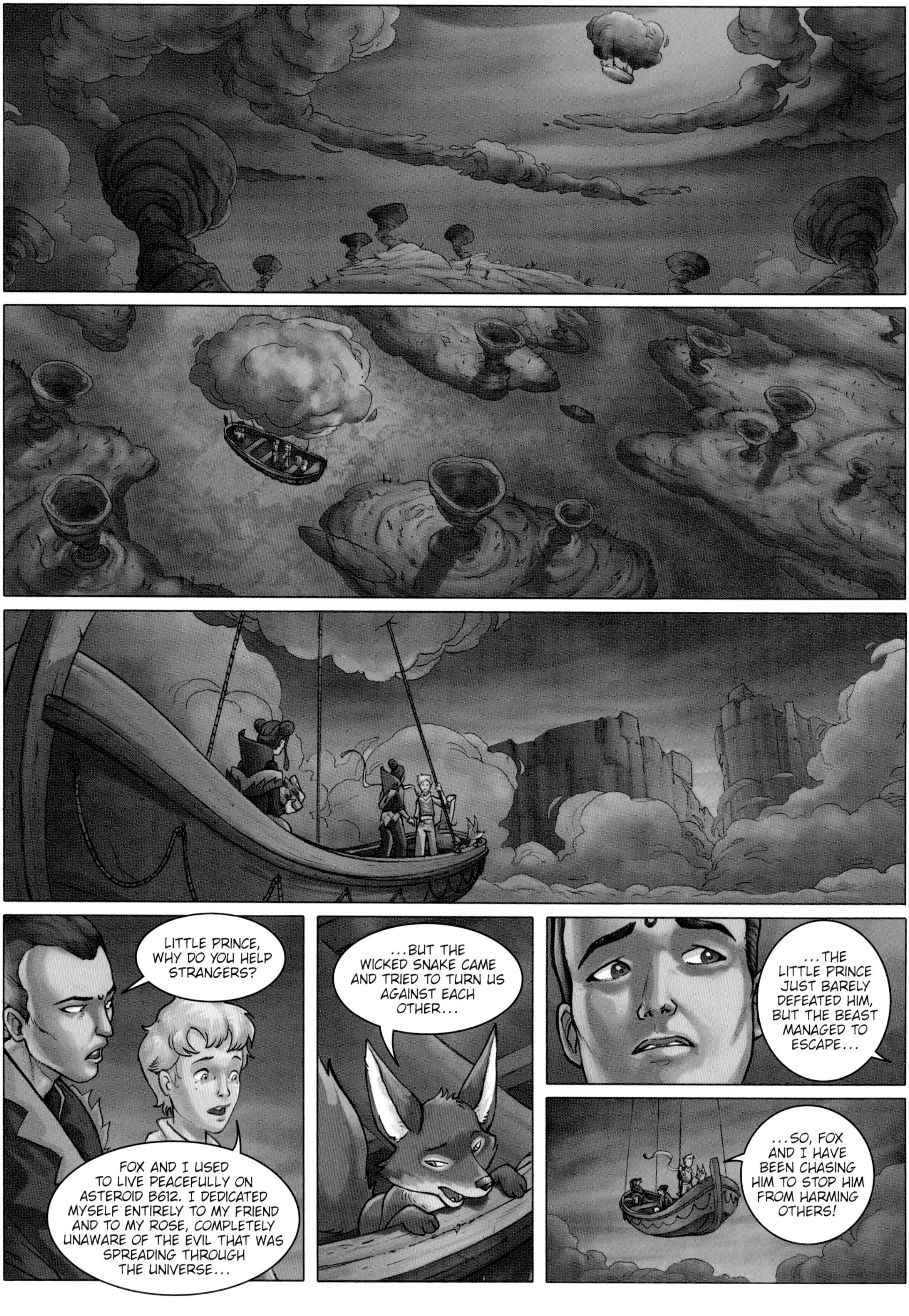
LITTLE PRINCE, WHY DO YOU HELP STRANGERS?
FOX AND I USED TO LIVE PEACEFULLY ON ASTEROID B612. I DEDICATED MYSELF ENTIRELY TO MY FRIEND AND TO MY ROSE, COMPLETELY UNAWARE OF THE EVIL THAT WAS SPREADING THROUGH THE UNIVERSE...
...BUT THE WICKED SNAKE CAME AND TRIED TO TURN US AGAINST EACH OTHER...
...THE LITTLE PRINCE JUST BARELY DEFEATED HIM, BUT THE BEAST MANAGED TO ESCAPE...
...SO, FOX AND I HAVE BEEN CHASING HIM TO STOP HIM FROM HARMING OTHERS!

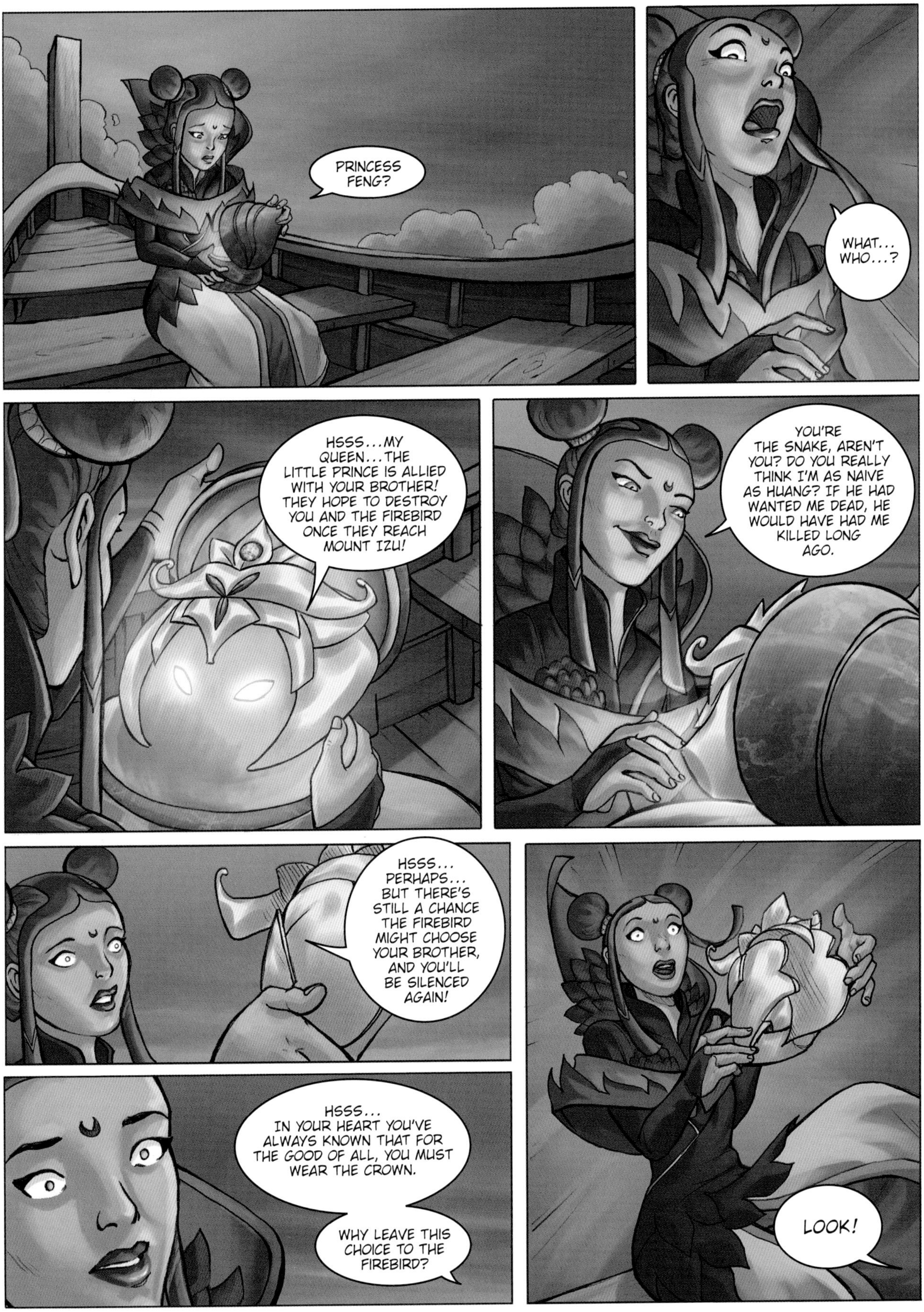

PRINCESS FENG?
WHAT... WHO...?
HSSS...MY QUEEN...THE LITTLE PRINCE IS ALLIED WITH YOUR BROTHER! THEY HOPE TO DESTROY YOU AND THE FIREBIRD ONCE THEY REACH MOUNT IZU!
YOU'RE THE SNAKE, AREN'T YOU? DO YOU REALLY THINK I'M AS NAIVE AS HUANG? IF HE HAD WANTED ME DEAD, HE WOULD HAVE HAD ME KILLED LONG AGO.
HSSS... PERHAPS... BUT THERE'S STILL A CHANCE THE FIREBIRD MIGHT CHOOSE YOUR BROTHER, AND YOU'LL BE SILENCED AGAIN!
HSSS... IN YOUR HEART YOU'VE ALWAYS KNOWN THAT FOR THE GOOD OF ALL, YOU MUST WEAR THE CROWN.
WHY LEAVE THIS CHOICE TO THE FIREBIRD?
LOOK!

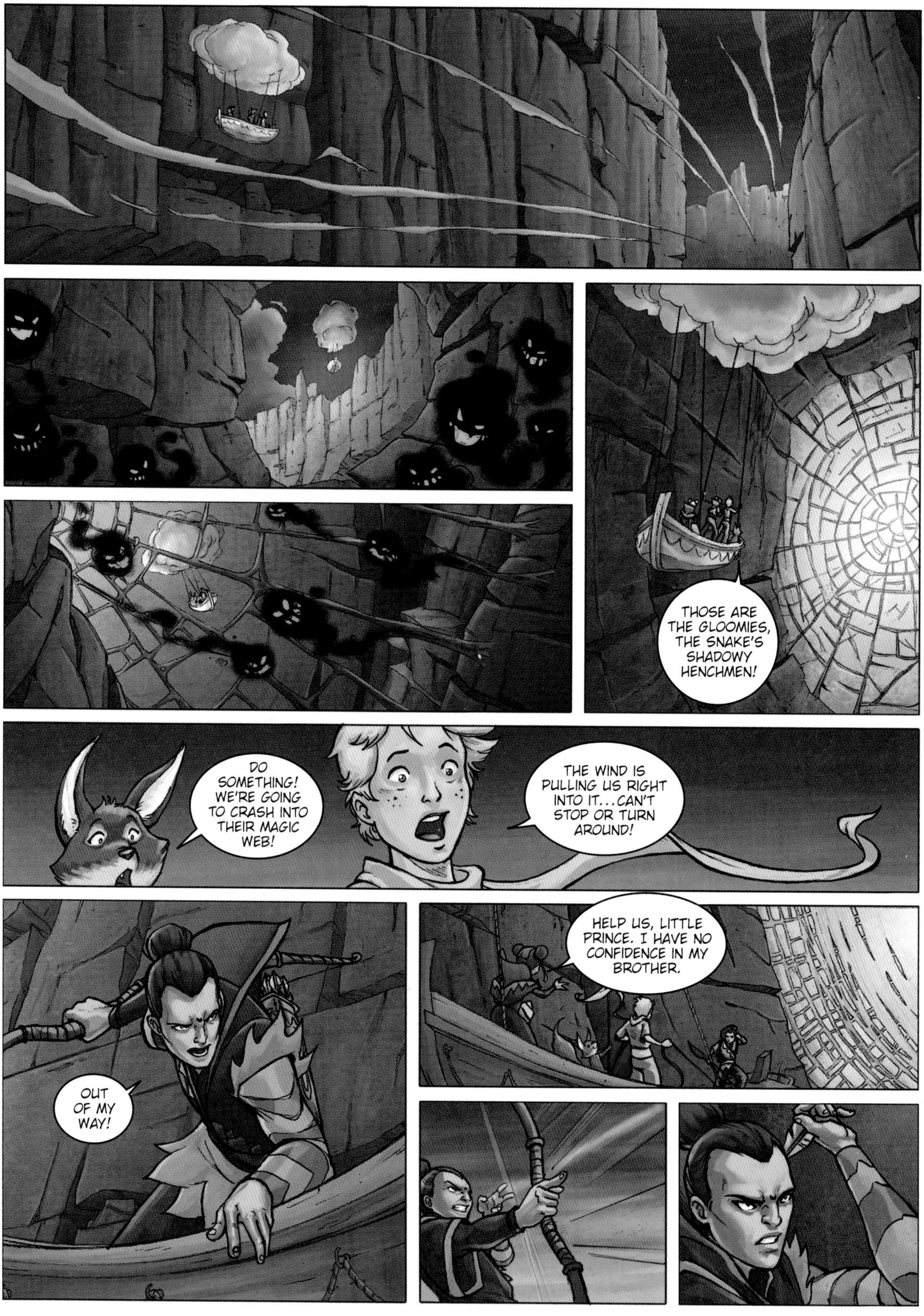
THOSE ARE THE GLOOMIES, THE SNAKE'S SHADOWY HENCHMEN!
DO SOMETHING! WE'RE GOING TO CRASH INTO THEIR MAGIC WEB!
THE WIND IS PULLING US RIGHT INTO IT... CAN'T STOP OR TURN AROUND!
OUT OF MY WAY!
HELP US, LITTLE PRINCE. I HAVE NO CONFIDENCE IN MY BROTHER.

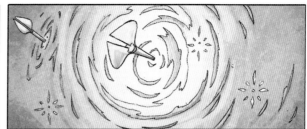

HE SAVED US, PRINCESS.

MOUNT IZU, AT LAST!

HURRY, IT'S ALMOST DAWN.

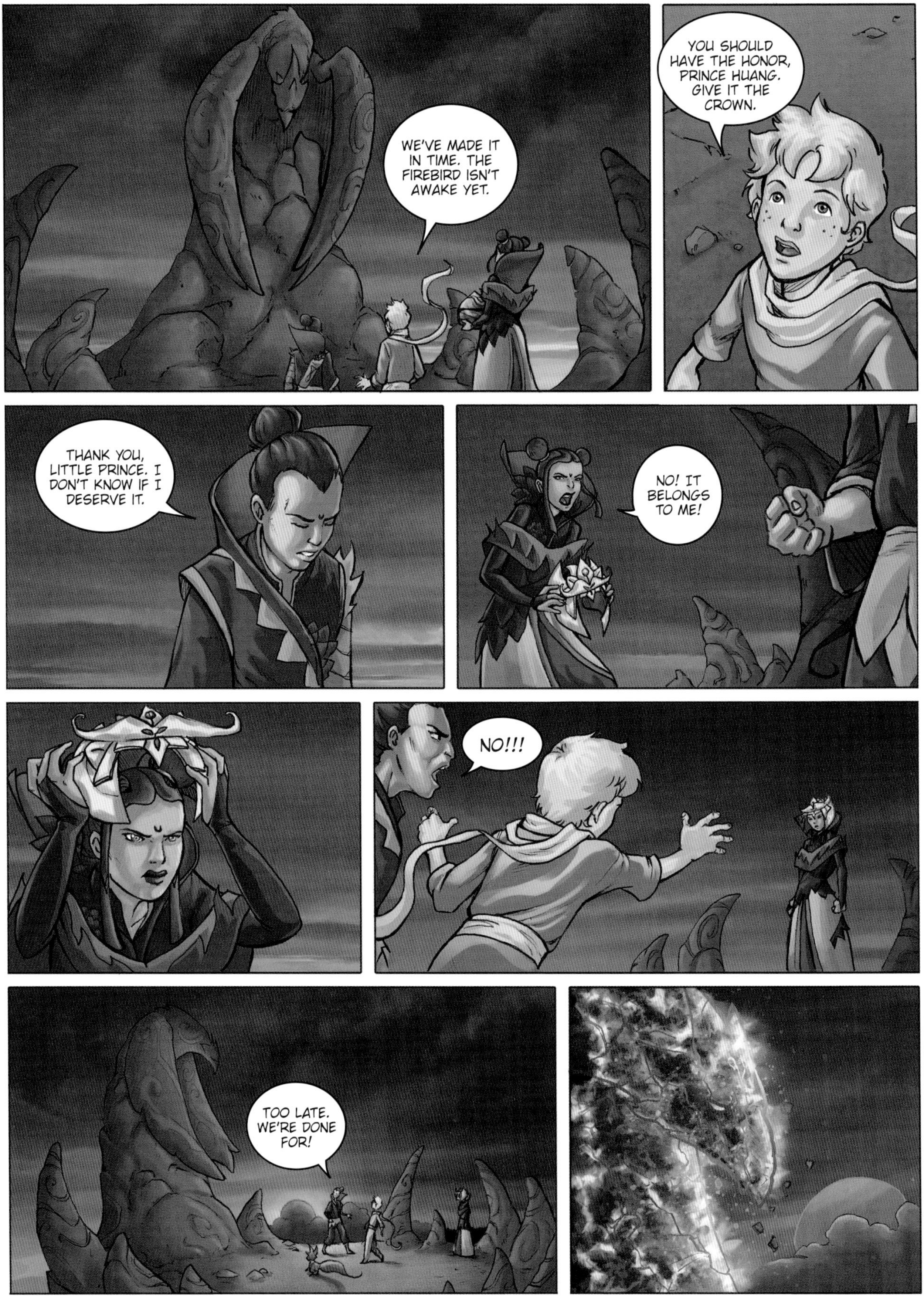
WE'VE MADE IT IN TIME. THE FIREBIRD ISN'T AWAKE YET.
YOU SHOULD HAVE THE HONOR, PRINCE HUANG. GIVE IT THE CROWN.
THANK YOU, LITTLE PRINCE. I DON'T KNOW IF I DESERVE IT.
NO! IT BELONGS TO ME!
NO!!!
TOO LATE. WE'RE DONE FOR!

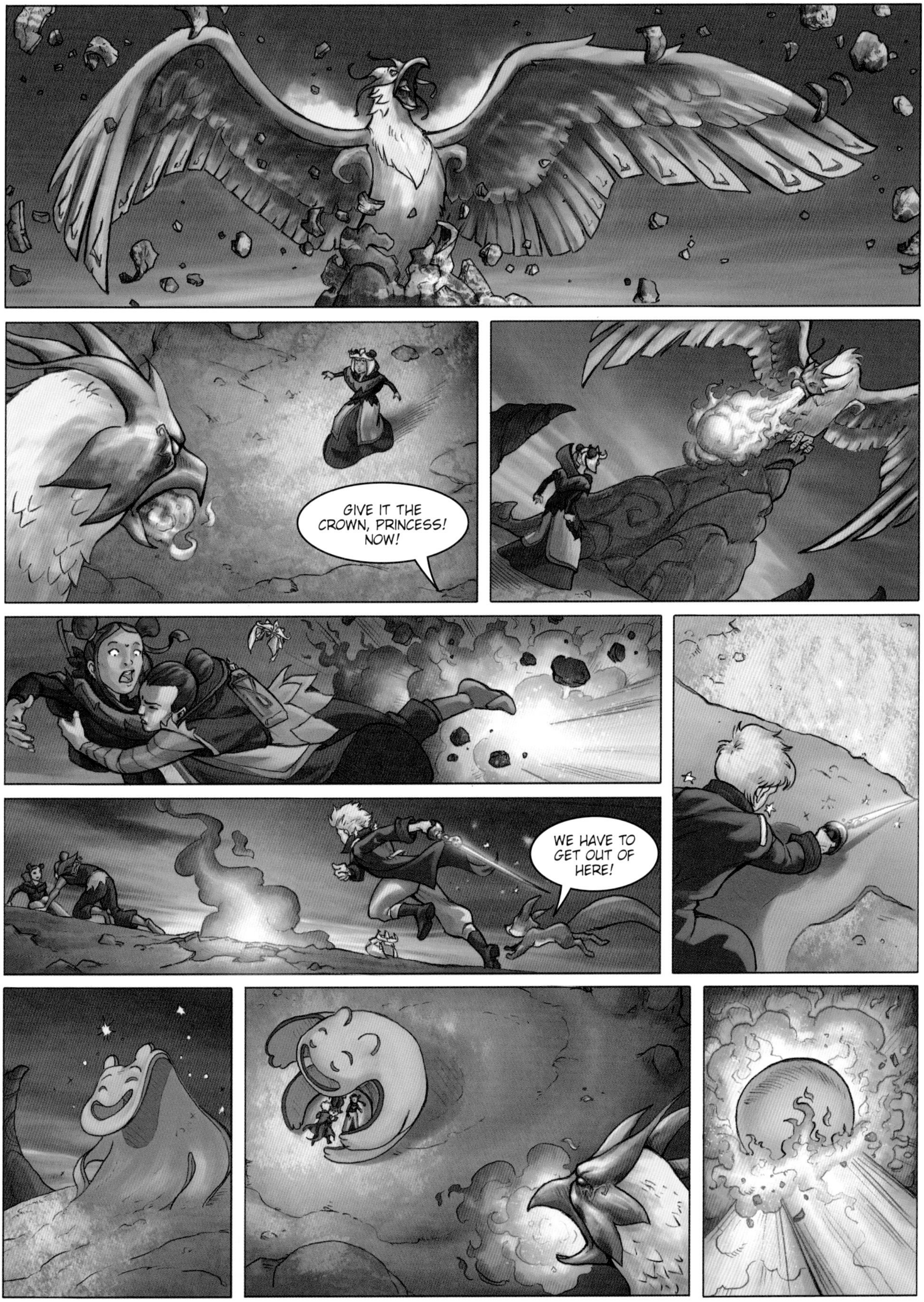
GIVE IT THE CROWN, PRINCESS! NOW!
WE HAVE TO GET OUT OF HERE!

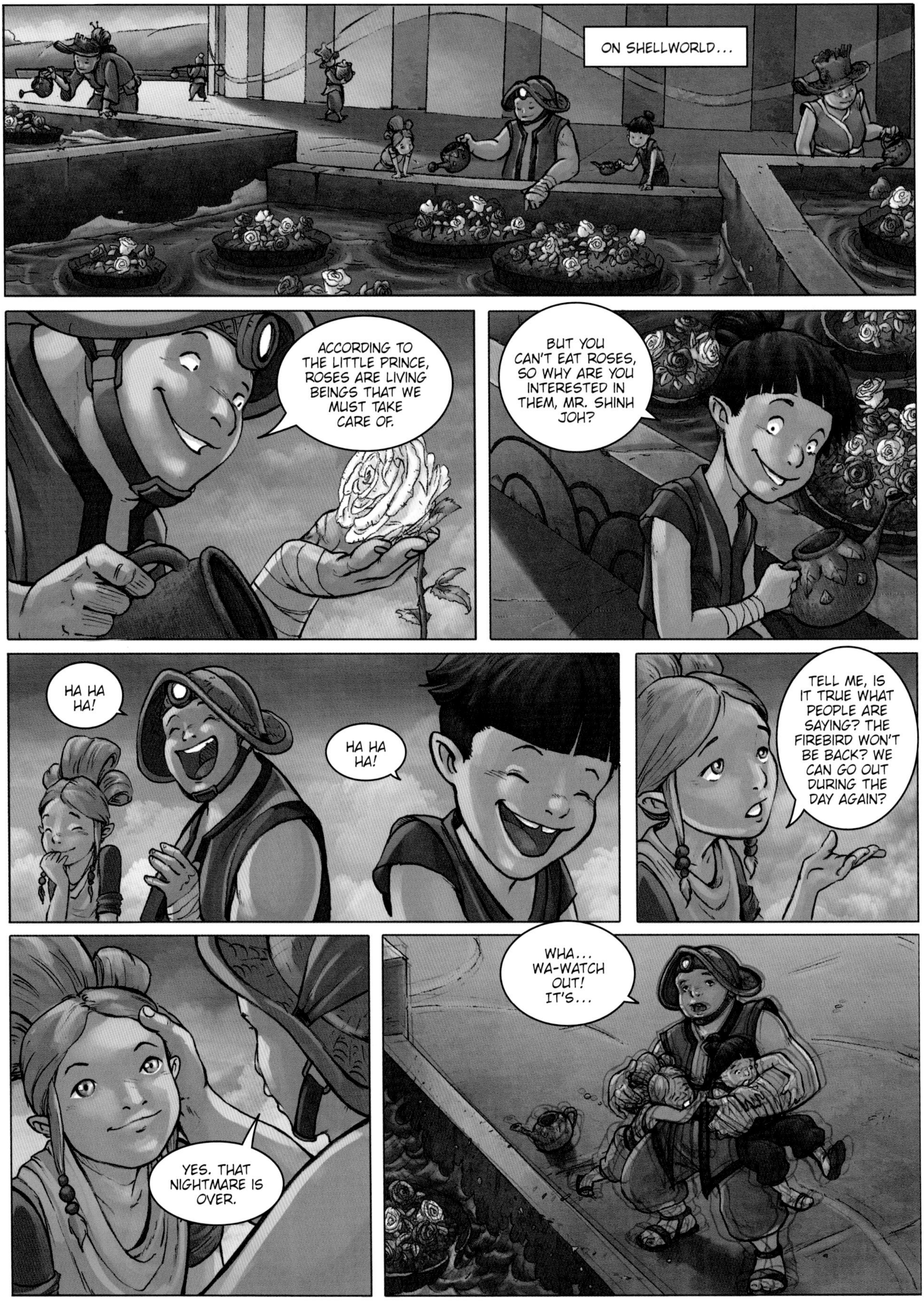
ON SHELLWORLD...
ACCORDING TO THE LITTLE PRINCE, ROSES ARE LIVING BEINGS THAT WE MUST TAKE CARE OF.
BUT YOU CAN'T EAT ROSES, SO WHY ARE YOU INTERESTED IN THEM, MR. SHINH JOH?
HA HA HA!
HA HA HA!
TELL ME, IS IT TRUE WHAT PEOPLE ARE SAYING? THE FIREBIRD WON'T BE BACK? WE CAN GO OUT DURING THE DAY AGAIN?
YES. THAT NIGHTMARE IS OVER.
WHA... WA-WATCH OUT! IT'S...

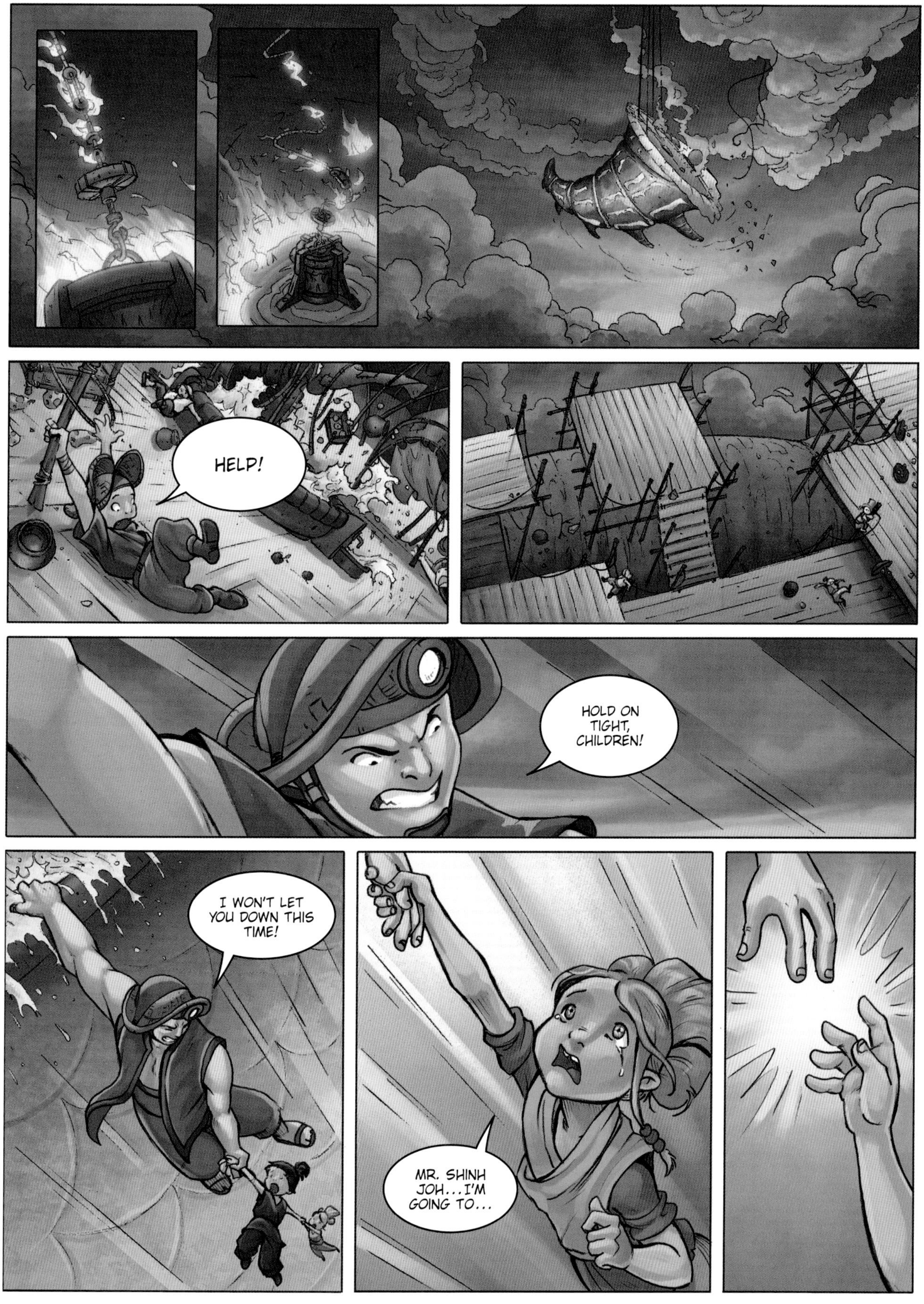
HELP!
HOLD ON TIGHT, CHILDREN!
I WON'T LET YOU DOWN THIS TIME!
MR. SHINH JOH...I'M GOING TO...

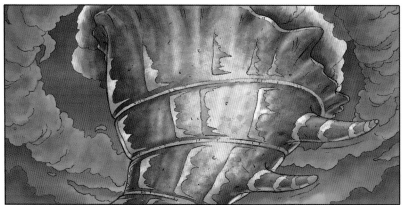

AAAAAAAH...

THANK YOU FOR HOLDING ON UNTIL WE GOT BACK, AND SORRY TO HAVE BEEN LATE!

BUT... HOW DID YOU STABILIZE SHELLWORLD?

ENJOYED YOUR RIDE?

IT'S ALL THANKS TO THE LITTLE PRINCE. AFTER WE MANAGED TO ESCAPE MOUNT IZU...

...WE FOLLOWED THE FIREBIRD HERE, AND THE LITTLE PRINCE USED HIS SKETCHBOOK TO CREATE SHEEP CLOUDS TO HOLD ONTO THE CITY'S DAMAGED CABLES.

WHY IS THE FIREBIRD STILL PUNISHING US?

DIDN'T YOU GIVE BACK THE CROWN?

THERE WERE SOME COMPLICATIONS...

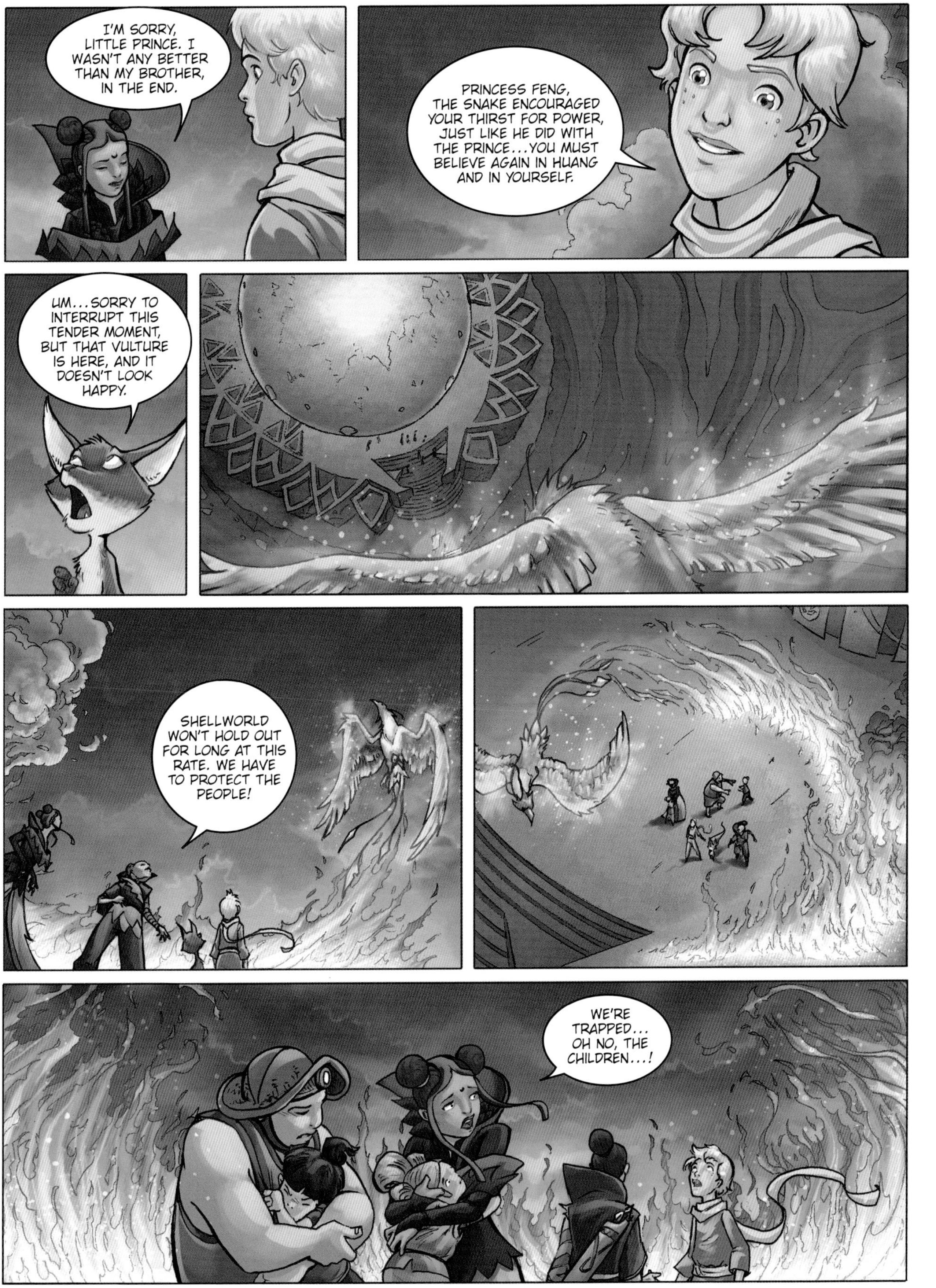
I'M SORRY, LITTLE PRINCE. I WASN'T ANY BETTER THAN MY BROTHER, IN THE END.
PRINCESS FENG, THE SNAKE ENCOURAGED YOUR THIRST FOR POWER, JUST LIKE HE DID WITH THE PRINCE...YOU MUST BELIEVE AGAIN IN HUANG AND IN YOURSELF.
UM...SORRY TO INTERRUPT THIS TENDER MOMENT, BUT THAT VULTURE IS HERE, AND IT DOESN'T LOOK HAPPY.
SHELLWORLD WON'T HOLD OUT FOR LONG AT THIS RATE. WE HAVE TO PROTECT THE PEOPLE!
WE'RE TRAPPED... OH NO, THE CHILDREN...!

HEY, LITTLE PRINCE, ARE YOU WAITING FOR AN INVITATION TO PLAY HERO?

I CAN'T...I ALREADY USED ALL MY STARDUST. I CAN'T USE MY SKETCHBOOK OR TRANSFORM MYSELF ANYMORE.

THEN IT'S UP TO ME TO SAVE SHELLWORLD. I'M GOING TO FIGHT IT!

THAT'S NOT THE ANSWER, PRINCE HUANG!

IN THE END, IT ONLY WANTS THE CROWN, RIGHT?

HERE IT IS, FIREBIRD. PLEASE FORGIVE US FOR STEALING IT FROM YOU!

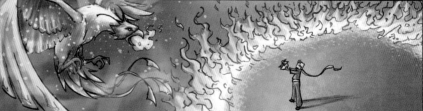

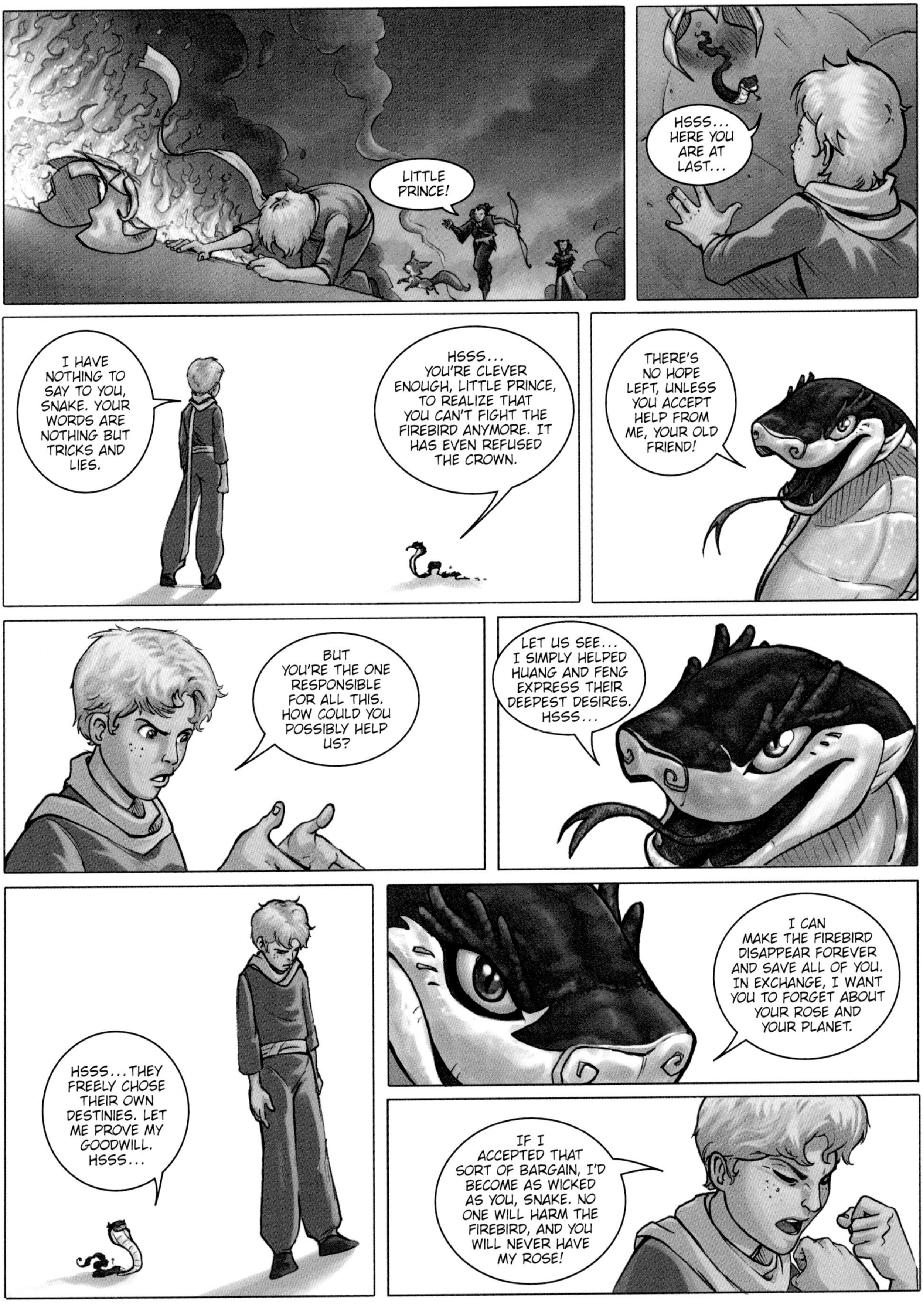
LITTLE PRINCE!
HSSS... HERE YOU ARE AT LAST...
I HAVE NOTHING TO SAY TO YOU, SNAKE. YOUR WORDS ARE NOTHING BUT TRICKS AND LIES.
HSSS... YOU'RE CLEVER ENOUGH, LITTLE PRINCE, TO REALIZE THAT YOU CAN'T FIGHT THE FIREBIRD ANYMORE. IT HAS EVEN REFUSED THE CROWN.
THERE'S NO HOPE LEFT, UNLESS YOU ACCEPT HELP FROM ME, YOUR OLD FRIEND!
BUT YOU'RE THE ONE RESPONSIBLE FOR ALL THIS. HOW COULD YOU POSSIBLY HELP US?
LET US SEE... I SIMPLY HELPED HUANG AND FENG EXPRESS THEIR DEEPEST DESIRES. HSSS...
HSSS...THEY FREELY CHOSE THEIR OWN DESTINIES. LET ME PROVE MY GOODWILL. HSSS...
I CAN MAKE THE FIREBIRD DISAPPEAR FOREVER AND SAVE ALL OF YOU. IN EXCHANGE, I WANT YOU TO FORGET ABOUT YOUR ROSE AND YOUR PLANET.
IF I ACCEPTED THAT SORT OF BARGAIN, I'D BECOME AS WICKED AS YOU, SNAKE. NO ONE WILL HARM THE FIREBIRD, AND YOU WILL NEVER HAVE MY ROSE!

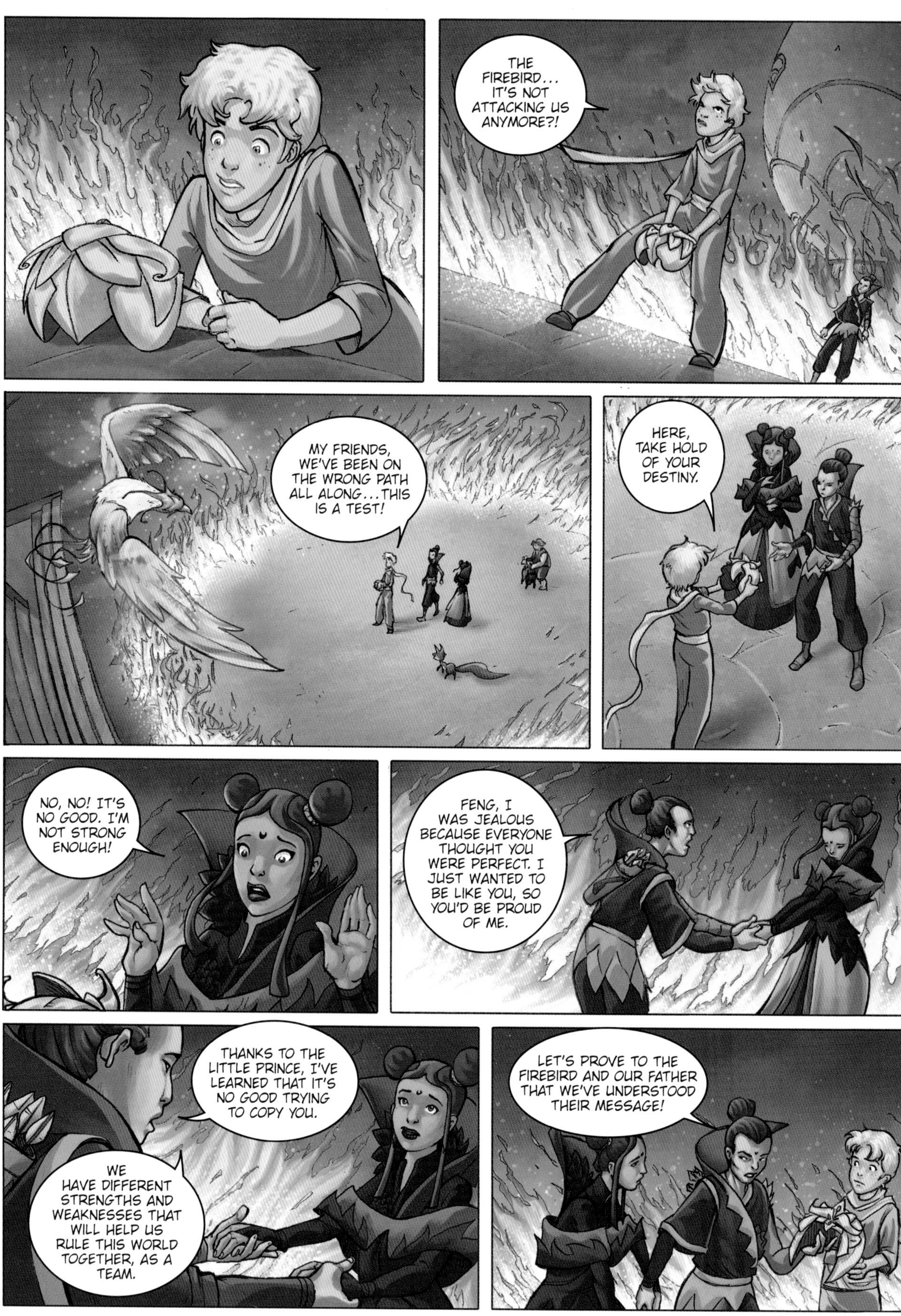

THE FIREBIRD... IT'S NOT ATTACKING US ANYMORE?!
MY FRIENDS, WE'VE BEEN ON THE WRONG PATH ALL ALONG... THIS IS A TEST!
HERE, TAKE HOLD OF YOUR DESTINY.
NO, NO! IT'S NO GOOD. I'M NOT STRONG ENOUGH!
FENG, I WAS JEALOUS BECAUSE EVERYONE THOUGHT YOU WERE PERFECT. I JUST WANTED TO BE LIKE YOU, SO YOU'D BE PROUD OF ME.
THANKS TO THE LITTLE PRINCE, I'VE LEARNED THAT IT'S NO GOOD TRYING TO COPY YOU.
WE HAVE DIFFERENT STRENGTHS AND WEAKNESSES THAT WILL HELP US RULE THIS WORLD TOGETHER, AS A TEAM.
LET'S PROVE TO THE FIREBIRD AND OUR FATHER THAT WE'VE UNDERSTOOD THEIR MESSAGE!

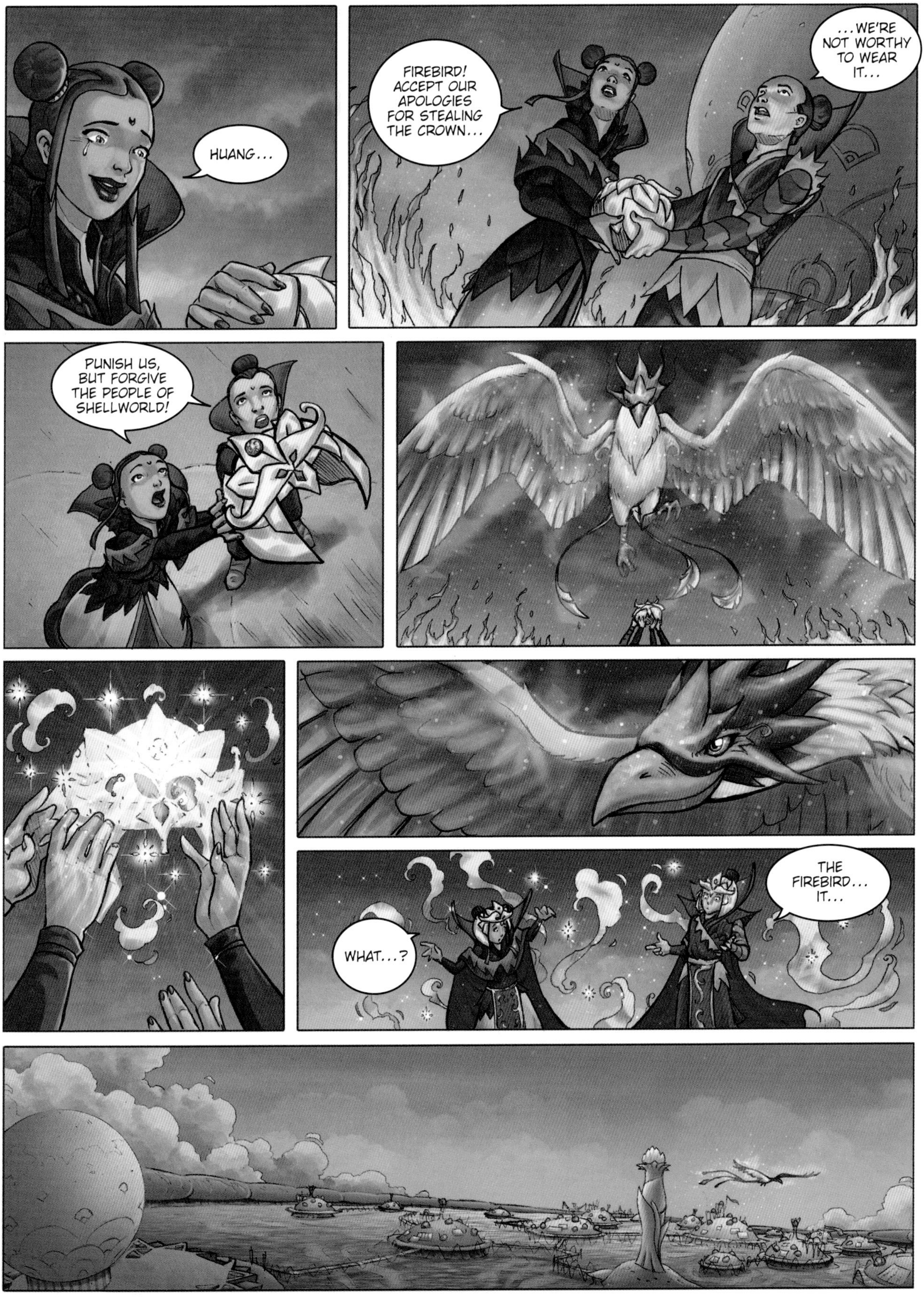
HUANG...
FIREBIRD! ACCEPT OUR APOLOGIES FOR STEALING THE CROWN...
...WE'RE NOT WORTHY TO WEAR IT...
PUNISH US, BUT FORGIVE THE PEOPLE OF SHELLWORLD!
WHAT...?
THE FIREBIRD... IT...

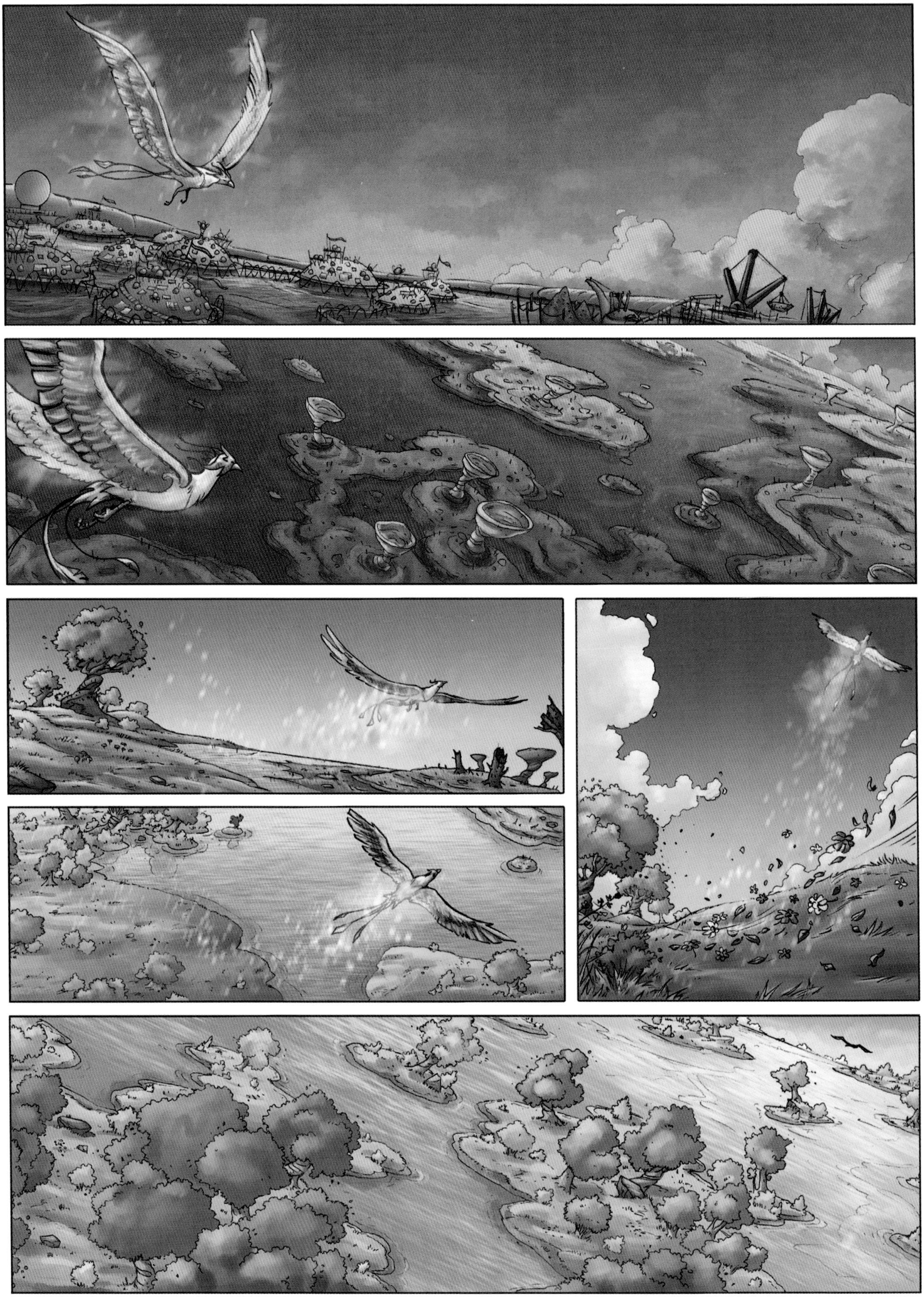

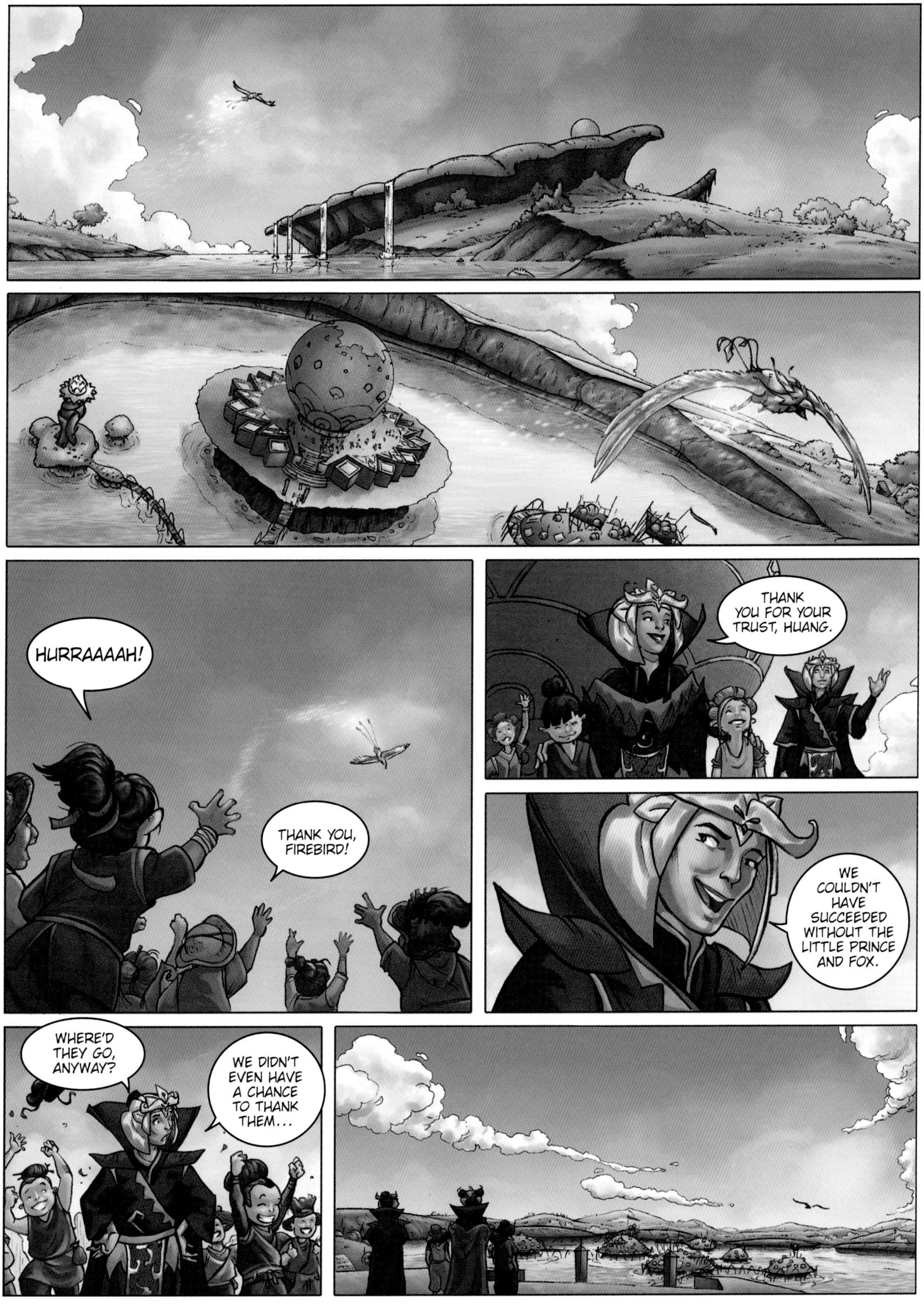
HURRAAAAH!
THANK YOU, FIREBIRD!
THANK YOU FOR YOUR TRUST, HUANG.
WE COULDN'T HAVE SUCCEEDED WITHOUT THE LITTLE PRINCE AND FOX.
WHERE'D THEY GO, ANYWAY?
WE DIDN'T EVEN HAVE A CHANCE TO THANK THEM...

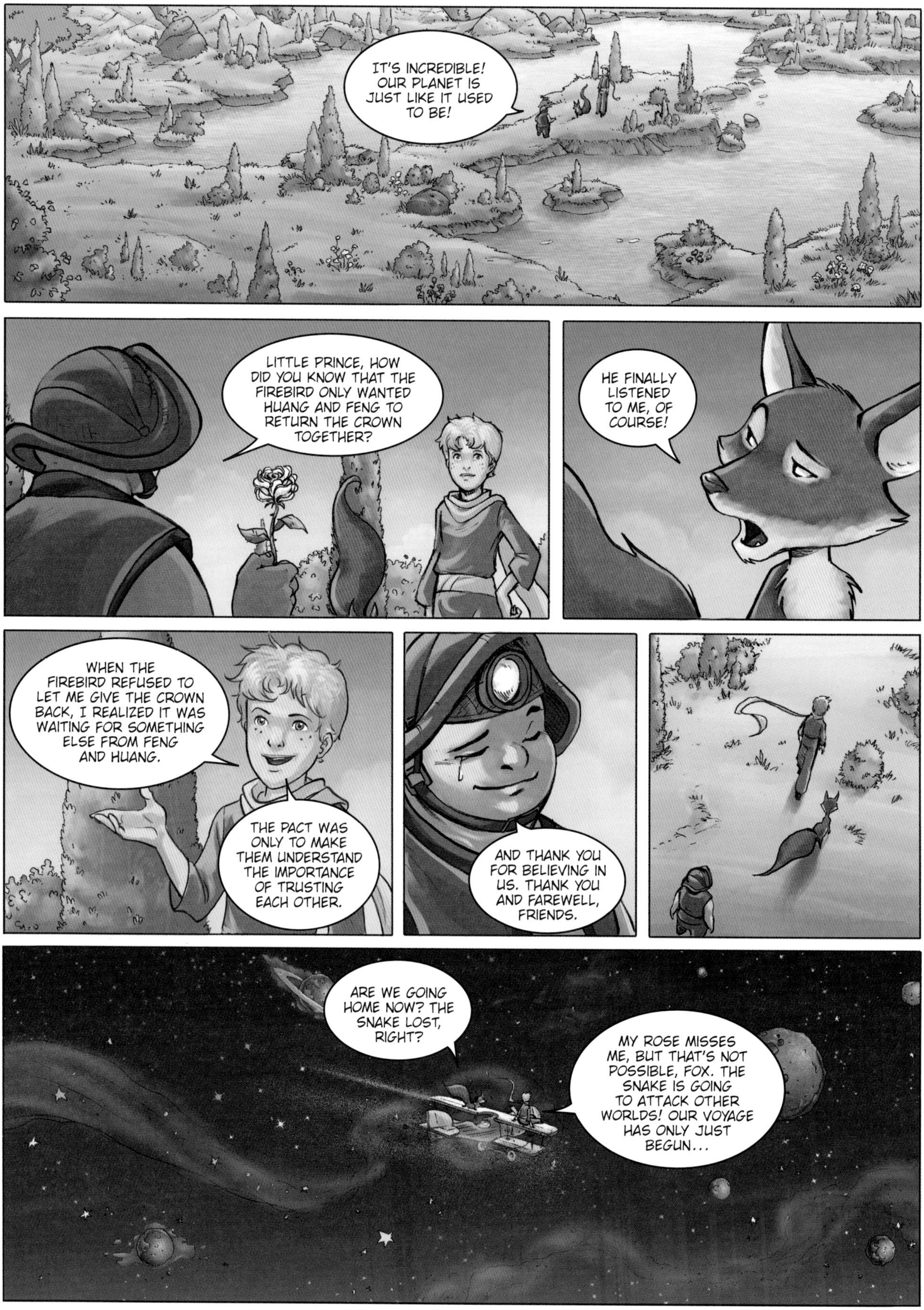
IT'S INCREDIBLE! OUR PLANET IS JUST LIKE IT USED TO BE!
LITTLE PRINCE, HOW DID YOU KNOW THAT THE FIREBIRD ONLY WANTED HUANG AND FENG TO RETURN THE CROWN TOGETHER?
HE FINALLY LISTENED TO ME, OF COURSE!
WHEN THE FIREBIRD REFUSED TO LET ME GIVE THE CROWN BACK, I REALIZED IT WAS WAITING FOR SOMETHING ELSE FROM FENG AND HUANG.
THE PACT WAS ONLY TO MAKE THEM UNDERSTAND THE IMPORTANCE OF TRUSTING EACH OTHER.
AND THANK YOU FOR BELIEVING IN US. THANK YOU AND FAREWELL, FRIENDS.
ARE WE GOING HOME NOW? THE SNAKE LOST, RIGHT?
MY ROSE MISSES ME, BUT THAT'S NOT POSSIBLE, FOX. THE SNAKE IS GOING TO ATTACK OTHER WORLDS! OUR VOYAGE HAS ONLY JUST BEGUN...

THE END

The Little Prince

AS IMAGINED BY
TEBO

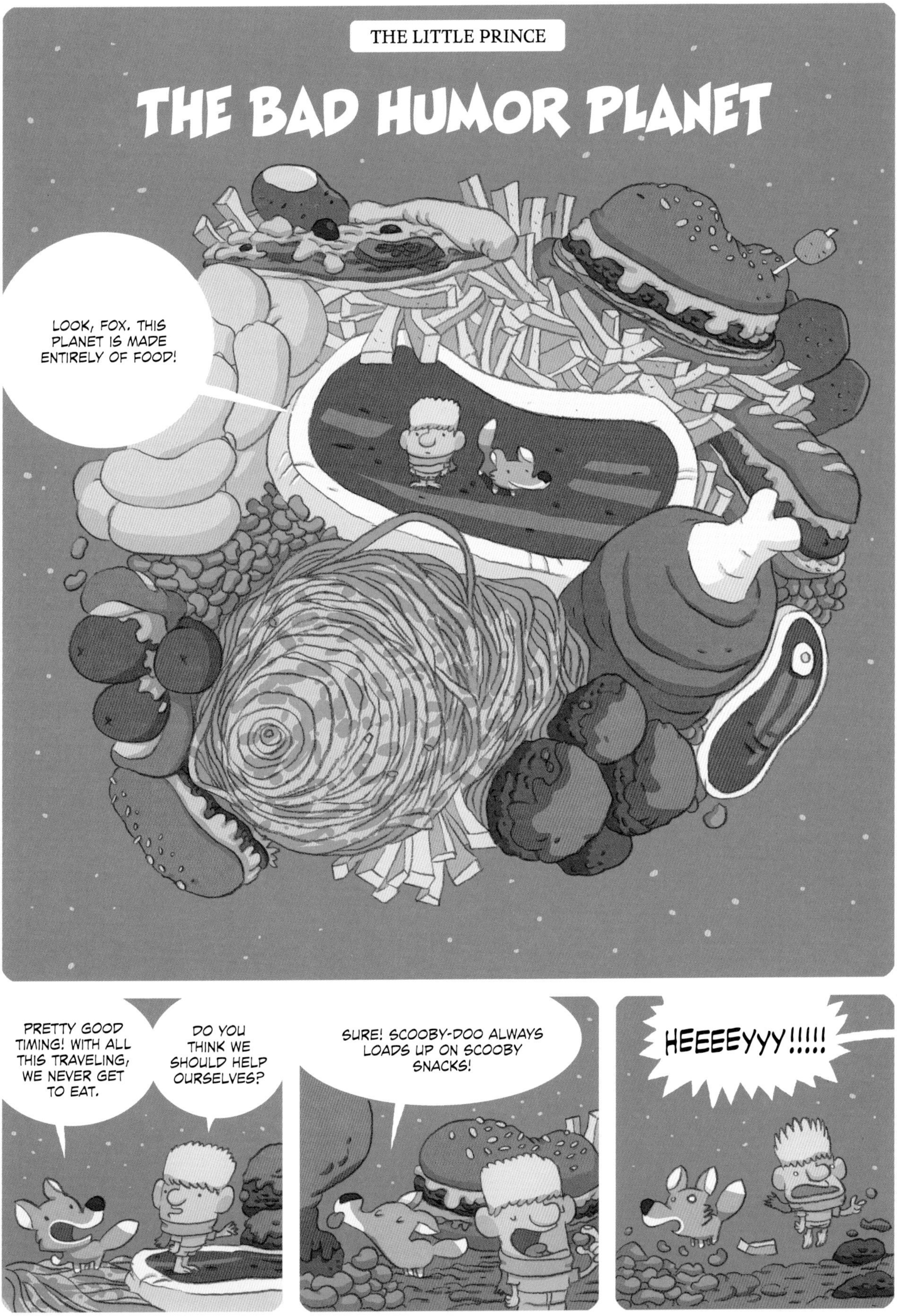
THE LITTLE PRINCE
THE BAD HUMOR PLANET
LOOK, FOX. THIS PLANET IS MADE ENTIRELY OF FOOD!
PRETTY GOOD TIMING! WITH ALL THIS TRAVELING, WE NEVER GET TO EAT.
DO YOU THINK WE SHOULD HELP OURSELVES?
SURE! SCOOBY-DOO ALWAYS LOADS UP ON SCOOBY SNACKS!
HEEEEyyy!!!!!

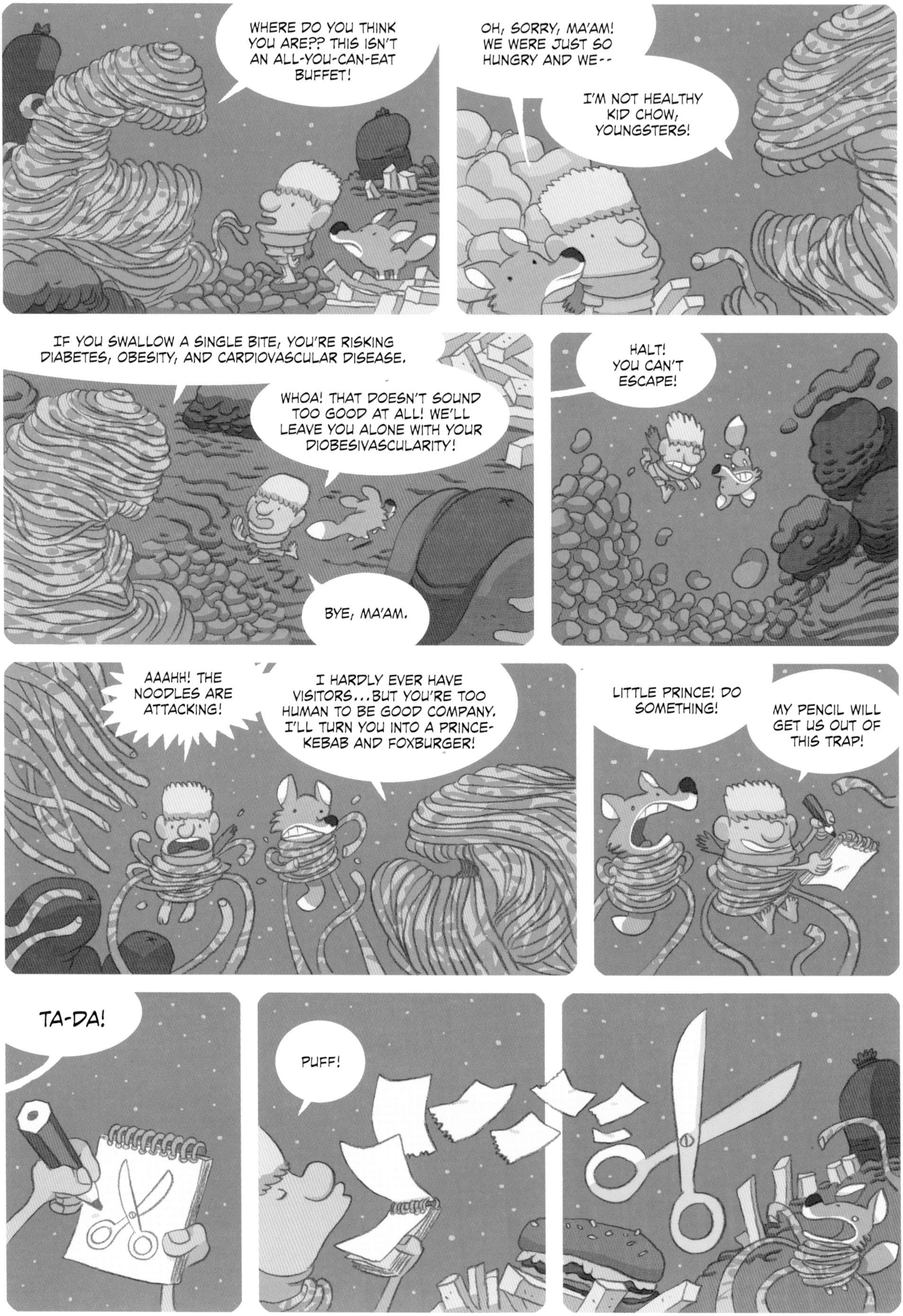
WHERE DO YOU THINK YOU ARE?? THIS ISN'T AN ALL-YOU-CAN-EAT BUFFET!
OH, SORRY, MA'AM! WE WERE JUST SO HUNGRY AND WE--
I'M NOT HEALTHY KID CHOW, YOUNGSTERS!
IF YOU SWALLOW A SINGLE BITE, YOU'RE RISKING DIABETES, OBESITY, AND CARDIOVASCULAR DISEASE.
WHOA! THAT DOESN'T SOUND TOO GOOD AT ALL! WE'LL LEAVE YOU ALONE WITH YOUR DIOBESIVASCULARITY!
BYE, MA'AM.
HALT! YOU CAN'T ESCAPE!
AAAHH! THE NOODLES ARE ATTACKING!
I HARDLY EVER HAVE VISITORS...BUT YOU'RE TOO HUMAN TO BE GOOD COMPANY. I'LL TURN YOU INTO A PRINCE-KEBAB AND FOXBURGER!
LITTLE PRINCE! DO SOMETHING!
MY PENCIL WILL GET US OUT OF THIS TRAP!
TA-DA!
PUFF!

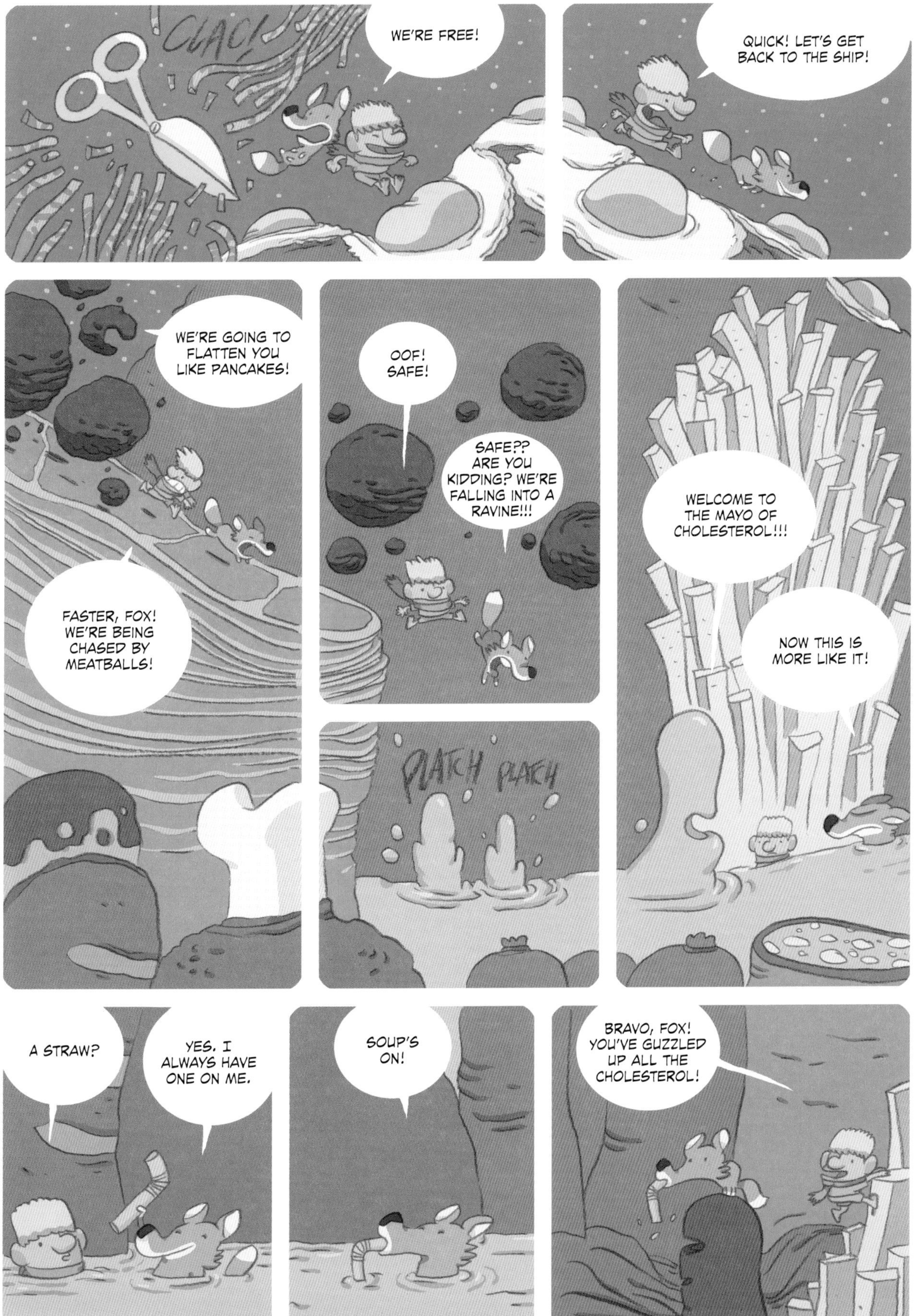
CLAC!
WE'RE FREE!
QUICK! LET'S GET BACK TO THE SHIP!
WE'RE GOING TO FLATTEN YOU LIKE PANCAKES!
FASTER, FOX! WE'RE BEING CHASED BY MEATBALLS!
OOF! SAFE!
SAFE?? ARE YOU KIDDING? WE'RE FALLING INTO A RAVINE!!!
PLATCH PLATCH
WELCOME TO THE MAYO OF CHOLESTEROL!!!
NOW THIS IS MORE LIKE IT!
A STRAW?
YES. I ALWAYS HAVE ONE ON ME.
SOUP'S ON!
BRAVO, FOX! YOU'VE GUZZLED UP ALL THE CHOLESTEROL!

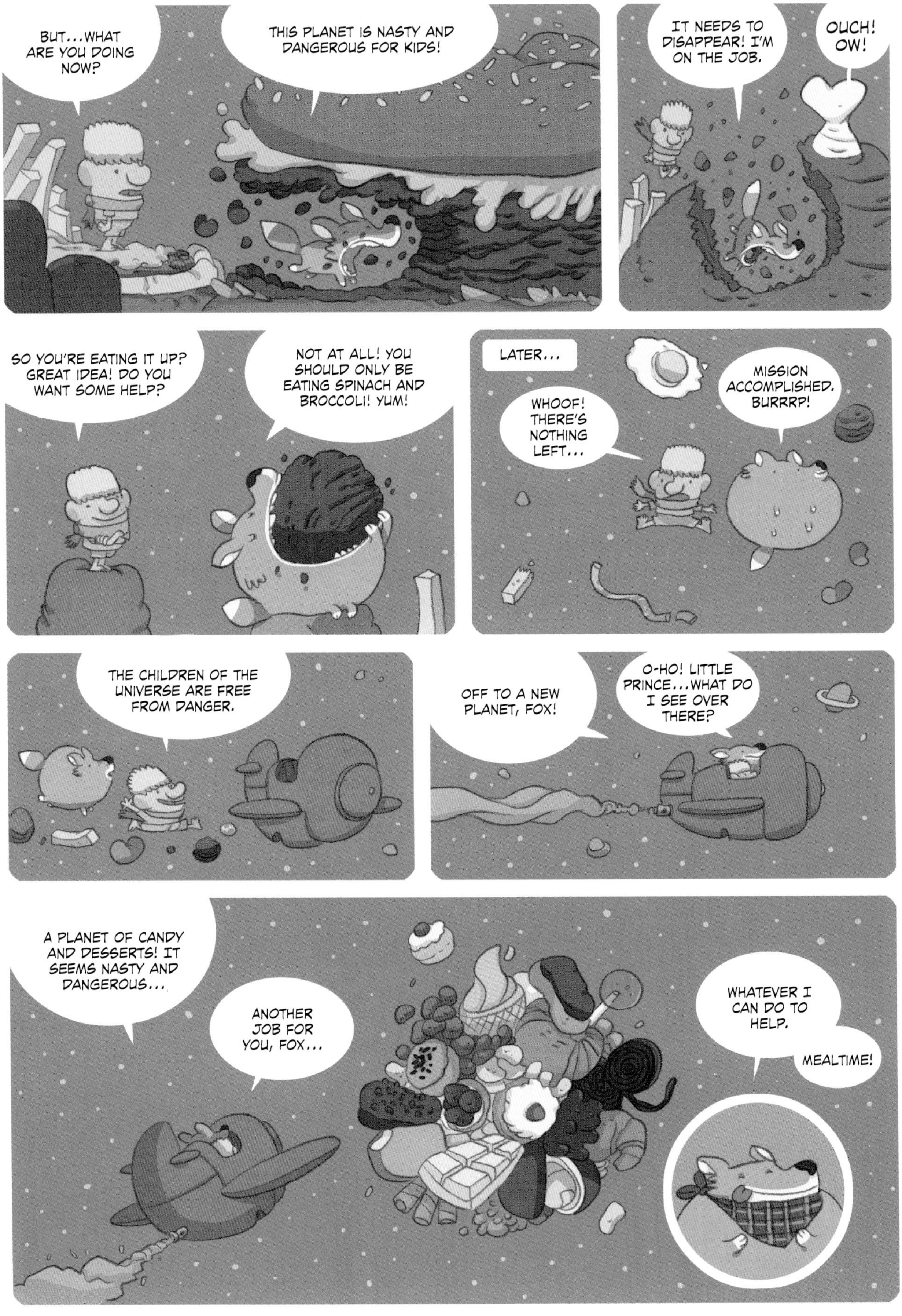
BUT...WHAT ARE YOU DOING NOW?
THIS PLANET IS NASTY AND DANGEROUS FOR KIDS!
IT NEEDS TO DISAPPEAR! I'M ON THE JOB.
OUCH! OW!
SO YOU'RE EATING IT UP? GREAT IDEA! DO YOU WANT SOME HELP?
NOT AT ALL! YOU SHOULD ONLY BE EATING SPINACH AND BROCCOLI! YUM!
LATER...
WHOOF! THERE'S NOTHING LEFT...
MISSION ACCOMPLISHED. BURRRP!
THE CHILDREN OF THE UNIVERSE ARE FREE FROM DANGER.
OFF TO A NEW PLANET, FOX!
O-HO! LITTLE PRINCE...WHAT DO I SEE OVER THERE?
A PLANET OF CANDY AND DESSERTS! IT SEEMS NASTY AND DANGEROUS...
ANOTHER JOB FOR YOU, FOX...
WHATEVER I CAN DO TO HELP.
MEALTIME!

The Little Prince
BOOK 1: THE PLANET OF WIND

The Little Prince
BOOK 2: THE PLANET OF THE FIREBIRD

The Little Prince
BOOK 3: THE PLANET OF MUSIC

The Little Prince
BOOK 4: THE PLANET OF JADE

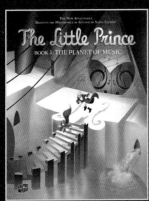

Book 1: The Planet of Wind

Book 2: The Planet of the Firebird

Book 3: The Planet of Music

Book 4: The Planet of Jade

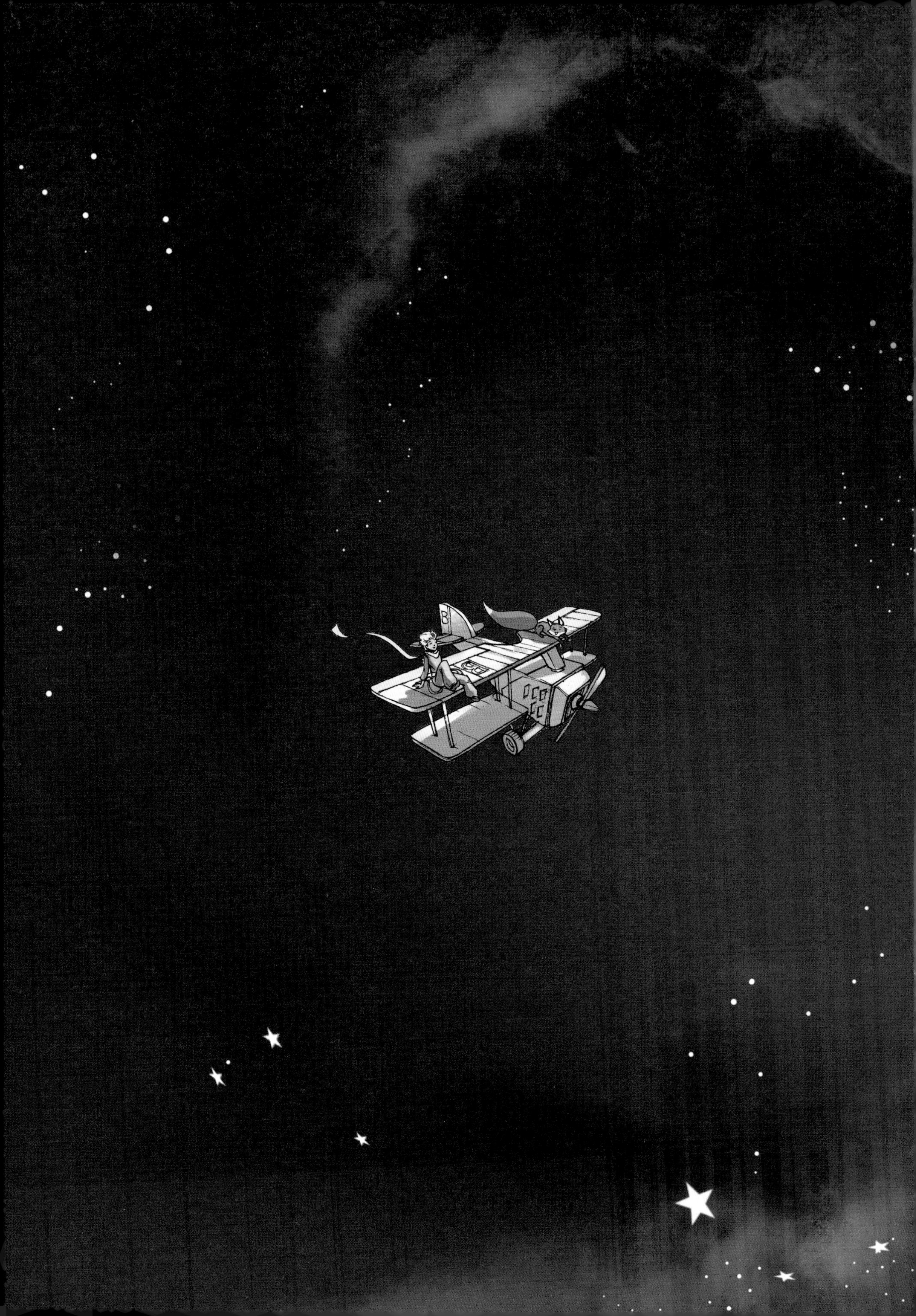